"Tell me, Dmitri," .... now, fully aware of what she was asking. No longer confused about her own want for him, no longer guilty or ashamed about it.

She'd never been an innocent, except in the most technical sense, anyway.

Still, Dmitri had given her a choice.

She wanted him, she had known that from the beginning. But tonight, there was no shame or weakness that came with that want. Tonight, there was nothing but the two of them.

"Because I realized the inevitability of this thing between us." His soft voice only amplified the spiraling tension in the room. "If not today, tomorrow. If not tomorrow...it's going to consume us both.

"I have never denied myself something I want. I want you. Every time you look at me, all I can think of is being inside you, every time you lash at me, all I can think of is kissing your mouth...

"To hell with your debt and my honor...to hell with pretending I'm something I'm not.

"Nothing in the past decade has made me as hungry or as desperate as you have, Jas.

"So, do you want this for as long as it will last? Do you have the guts to actually take me on, Jas? Because if I touch you, I won't stop."

Greek Tycoons Tamed

When power and pride are undone by passion!

Stavros Sporades and Dmitri Karegas are renowned throughout the world as Greece's most powerful and determined tycoons!

But have these untouchable Greek tycoons finally met the women who can tame them?

Find out in...

Stavros and Leah's story:
Claimed for His Duty
August 2015

The wife Stavros hasn't seen for nearly five years is back and demanding a divorce! But Stavros isn't about to let his errant wife escape from his grasp... they have unfinished business!

Dmitri and Jasmine's story:
Bought for Her Innocence
November 2015

Dmitri is known for the women who visit his bed as much as the millions in his bank account. So when a childhood friend auctions her innocence, Dmitri intends to be the highest bidder!

Tara Pammi

Bought for Her Innocence

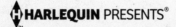

Recycling programs
for this product may
not exist in your area.

ISBN-13: 978-0-373-13390-1

Bought for Her Innocence

First North American Publication 2015

Copyright © 2015 by Tara Pammi

Printed in U.S.A.

Tara Pammi can't remember a moment when she wasn't lost in a book—especially a romance, which was much more exciting than a mathematics textbook. Years later, Tara's wild imagination and love for the written word revealed what she really wanted to do. Now she pairs alpha males who think they know everything with strong women who knock that theory *and* them off their feet!

Books by Tara Pammi

Harlequin Presents

The Man to Be Reckoned With
A Deal with Demakis

Greek Tycoons Tamed

Claimed for His Duty

Society Weddings

The Sicilian's Surprise Wife

A Dynasty of Sand and Scandal

The Last Prince of Dahaar
The True King of Dahaar

The Sensational Stanton Sisters

A Hint of Scandal
A Touch of Temptation

Visit the Author Profile page
at Harlequin.com for more titles.

CHAPTER ONE

"I HAVE A proposition for you, Jasmine, that would allow you to pay off your brother's debt within a year."

Fear was a cold fist clamped over her spine, but Jasmine Douglas forced herself to stare steadily into the chilly green eyes of Noah King.

That word *proposition* from any other man of her acquaintance, while wholly unwelcome but an awful reality of her life, was something she was used to.

The clientele of the club where she worked, owned by Noah, was constantly under the impression that her scantily clad, gyrating-around-a-pole body was up for sale. That *she* was for sale.

She wasn't and never would be.

Only soul-wrenching fear of the consequences of owing a debt to this man who owned three underground gambling clubs in London, and who was even now contemplating her future without blinking, had forced her into it.

She had barely buried her brother Andrew when she had learned of the debt he had piled up with *Noah King*, of all people. Desperation to resolve this debt and a need for survival forced her every night to take the stage.

So coming from Noah, that dangerous word turned the very blood in her veins into ice. "I've not missed a single payment, Noah," she finally said through a dry mouth.

"Yes, but you're barely making a dent. You have no assets that you could sell off, either."

Her skin turned cold in the comfortably warm warehouse that was the headquarters of Noah's empire. A couple of completely harmless-looking men had showed up at her flat this morning and very politely accompanied her to see Noah here.

Sweat pooling over her neck, Jasmine realized how foolish she was to assume that anything related to Noah King was harmless.

"Am I a prisoner, then?" she said, before she could hold back the reckless question.

Noah didn't even blink as he casually peeled an orange and offered her some. "Until we find a satisfactory resolution, yes."

Her gut dropped and she fought the instinct to turn around and run. No phrase had ever scared the daylights out of her like *satisfactory resolution*.

Why, oh, why hadn't Andrew thought of where his debt would lead him one day? How could he have left her to deal with this dangerous man?

How, after all the promises he had made to her, could he have left her even worse than they had already been?

She had slaved for five years and was still stuck in this man's power, like a fly stuck in a spider's web. The more she tried to get out, the more she was ensnared.

On the heels of that thought came instant guilt. Andrew's face flashed in front of her, his eagerness shining in his eyes, his expression so kind, lodging a lump in her throat.

We'll get out of this dump one day, Jas. You just wait and watch. I'll get us out of here.

Her brother had only wanted what was best for her, had only wanted to improve their lot in life. Had watched out for her for years.

Equipped with no skills, saddled with their mother's

drinking and responsibility for Jas, he had seen no other way out of the hellhole they had been born into except by trying his luck in Noah's gambling den.

Not his fault that he had died so suddenly at only twenty-nine in an accident. Not his fault that everyone they had counted on had disappointed them.

And just like that, as though he was a thorn forever lodged under her skin, like a memory that had been burned into her brain, Dmitri came to mind.

Dmitri Karegas—godson of Giannis Katrakis, textile tycoon and internationally renowned playboy, collector of expensive toys like yachts and Bugattis and...*beautiful women.*

Dmitri, who had grown up along with them on the streets of London after his English father's business went into bankruptcy, whom Andrew had shielded from his alcoholic father numerous times, Dmitri, whom Andrew had treated like a brother, Dmitri, to whom Andrew had gone in need and who had refused to help an old friend while he led a filthy rich life, who had looked at her so coldly at Andrew's funeral and offered her cash.

Dmitri, whose exploits she followed with something bordering on obsession.

Thinking of Andrew would only weaken her; thinking of the man who might have helped was definitely a certain waste of her energies now.

It was as if there was glass in her throat as she looked back at Noah. "How much do I owe?"

"Thirty thousand pounds. It would take you another decade to pay it off if you continue as you do. But if you added a little something more personal to your menu at the club, then I see this going somewhere. You're a huge hit, Jasmine, and I've been getting offer after offer..."

Noah's words came as if from a distance, as if it was

happening to some other person, as if it was the only way her mind could deal with it… Sweat gathered over her forehead and the back of her neck, the pungent odor of alcohol and sweaty bodies that clung to the walls of the warehouse cutting off her breath.

The only thing that did burn into her mind was that she would be one step closer to selling herself, if not all the way. That was what Noah had decided for her. If she didn't get out now, she never would.

But how? Her lungs burned with the effort to draw breath; her knees locked in utter fear.

"…unless someone offers to buy out your debt, you have no choice." Noah's words floated into her mind again.

That was it. That was all she needed—someone to pay off her debt, to buy her from Noah.

And that someone had to be Dmitri.

No, that ashamed part of her screamed. If she went to him for help, he would know how low she had fallen. He would…

Better to sell herself to a known devil than an unknown one, the rational part of her asserted.

But even Dmitri couldn't just extract her from Noah King with all the power he had amassed. Not after he had turned his back on this life and everything in it.

Not if he had become a soft man who spent his days lounging about on his yacht and nights with women who did his every bidding.

Jasmine would have to provide Dmitri an opening and pray that he would take the bait. And if he didn't, the consequences didn't bear thinking about.

The article she had seen in the tech magazine that had been wrapped around the loaf of warm bread she had bought at the bakery only last week came to her. She had nothing to lose at this point and still, everything to gain.

"Put my virginity up for an auction," she said loudly,

the words burning her lips. "Give me a chance to pay it off at once."

A deafening silence filled the hall. Jasmine could feel ten sets of eyes on her, her skin crawling at the obviously male interest in her. Steadily, she held Noah's gaze, immensely grateful that at least his gaze was free of the openly nauseating lust she usually found herself the target of.

But then, Noah was, first and always, a businessman.

His silent appraisal of her gave Jasmine hope. Her breath ballooned up in her chest, crushing her lungs as she waited for his reply.

"You think someone will buy you," he finally said, a greedy glint in his eye. She had caught his interest, she realized, a shaky relief filling her inside out.

"Yes," she said, putting all her confidence in that single word. "Give me a week, Noah, please," she added, desperation coating her throat.

"Three days," Noah finally said.

A shake of his head had one of his thugs accompanying Jasmine to the room she had been brought to earlier.

For a second, Jasmine shook violently from head to toe, utter fear drenching her.

No, she couldn't lose her nerve now.

Switching her prepaid cell phone on, Jasmine clicked the number she had memorized years ago on the clunky keys, every breath coming like a chore. It had been years; he wouldn't probably have the same number anymore.

Even if he did have it, he might not care.

Pressing the cold phone to her forehead, Jasmine held back the hot sting of tears.

This had to work.

She backspaced a few times as her fingers shook on the phone screen. Her stomach tight, her hands clammy, she hit Send and crumpled against the floor.

* * *

In the process of putting his discarded shirt on, Dmitri Karegas flicked a glance toward the blonde provocatively stretched over his bed.

"Come back to bed," she whispered without any fabricated coyness.

What was her name? Mandy? Maddie?

For the life of him, Dmitri couldn't remember such a simple thing. And couldn't manage any shame over it, either.

Work, party, sex—these were the parameters of his life. He didn't hate women, didn't remember deciding to make his life so. But there it was.

He had worked around the clock for the past two months, trying to undo the damage his business partner and oldest friend, Stavros, had wreaked on Katrakis Textiles' stock with his uncharacteristic behavior, and finalizing a coup that had finally landed a nightclub he had been dying to acquire on his portfolio.

So he had found the blonde at the nightclub on his first night looking over his new toy.

She was everything he liked in a woman—willing, wanton, with a wicked tongue to boot. Even better, she didn't fill the silence with inane chatter and hadn't even dropped those usual hints about a budding relationship.

One creamy thigh bared as she slid upward in the bed. Yet as her rose-colored nipples puckered into tight buds under his continued stare, all he felt was an echo of arousal, the way a dog would lift its muzzle at the scent of meat.

Nothing else. Just like the numerous times over the past decade.

He worked, he collected his toys, he slept with willing women, yet somehow Dmitri never felt anything but a surface reaction, as if he was skimming through the very edge of life, incapable of sinking beneath the surface, forever on the outsides of it.

As if what he had turned off all those years ago to live through another day could never be turned on again. Even when he had helped Anya, who had become a sort of a friend, it had been a shallow echo of a different reality, another life where he had saved his mother that night.

Laughter, gravelly and as shocking as if a mountain rose in the midst of the sea, reached his ears, cutting off his unnerving reverie.

It was the afternoon that Leah had invited Stavros and herself to lunch aboard his yacht.

Looking around, he found his jeans and pulled them on.

He had always liked his godfather's granddaughter. But ever since Leah and Stavros had found their way to each other, which he had been damn glad about because all the drama around their marriage had caused the Katrakis Textiles' stock to sink, he had begun finding it distinctly uneasy to be in their company.

He knew what the source of that unease was but he was damned if he gave it voice. Neither did he feel up to the disapproving glance that would come from Stavros.

Even though he was only older by three years, Stavros treated him as if Dmitri was still the sixteen-year-old thug that their godfather Giannis had brought to his estate.

"Leave as soon as you can," he told the woman without meeting her gaze.

As soon as he stepped on the upper deck, Leah pulled away from Stavros and gave him a loose hug. "It's good to see you, Dmitri."

The familiar warmth of her slender body chased a sudden shiver through him, as shocking as if a cavern of emotion had opened up amongst the emptiness. Something must have flickered in his face because Stavros studied him closely.

Ever since Stavros had accepted that he was in love with Leah, after years of scorning Dmitri for what he called his reckless, hedonistic lifestyle, Stavros knew how empty Dmitri felt inside.

"I liked you better before," he said roughly, warning Stavros away.

Leah looked between them, frowning. "What?"

"Nothing," Stavros delivered in a flat tone. The knot of his gut relented a little and Dmitri breathed easy, slipping into the mode of that reckless playboy that was bone-deep now.

He pulled a chair for Leah and signaled to his staff to serve lunch. Pulling on a practiced smile, he looked at Leah. "So what has prompted you two to emerge from your love nest a week before the wedding?"

Leah sighed. "I would like for you to give me away at the wedding. Giannis is not here and you mean a lot to me, Dmitri."

"How many more times do I have to give you away?" he teased while intensely glad that she had asked him.

Her gaze twinkling, Leah grabbed Stavros's hand and laced her fingers through his. "Just this one more time."

After years of shouldering duty and knowing nothing but rules, Stavros had finally found a measure of happiness with Leah.

Holding Stavros's gaze, because he would die rather than betray anything else that he might be feeling to his friend, Dmitri said, "It will be my pleasure, Leah."

The sharp chime of his cell phone drew his attention. Frowning at the strange number, he clicked it.

I need help, Dmitri. Call Noah and find out. Do this for Andrew.

A cold nail raking over his spine, Dmitri stared at the message.

Images and sensations—his father's drunken rages, his mother's tired face, his own powerlessness, stinking alleys filled with Dumpsters, fistfights and broken noses, sobbing when Andrew held him hard, and a girl with huge, dark eyes in her oval face…

Jasmine…

Christos, the message is from Jasmine.

His gut clenched so hard that he pushed at the table and stood with a growl, a violence of emotion he hadn't known in years holding him in its feral grip.

Noah… Noah King… The man who ruled over the lowlifes of London like a king ran his empire… Lending and extortion, bars and nightclubs, pimps and prostitution, there was no pie that Noah didn't have a finger in.

And Jasmine was caught in it.

A soft hand on his arm brought him back from the pounding fury… He turned to see Leah staring at him with such shock that his breath burst into him in a wild rush.

On his other side stood Stavros, his gaze filled with concern. "Dmitri, who was that text from?"

"Jasmine." Even saying her name sent a pulse of something through Dmitri. As if he was opening a door he had closed on the worst night of his life. As if he was suddenly a spiraling vortex of emotion instead of empty inside.

"Jasmine, as in Andrew's sister?" Stavros's understanding was instant.

"Yes, she is in trouble," he replied, running his hand through his hair.

His muscles pumped with the need for action; he wanted to smash something, he…

"Dmitri, let's discuss what needs to be done," Stavros interjected calmly, as if aware of how raw he felt. Of course, his friend knew.

He opened the message and read it again. He had thought Jasmine better off without his interest and instead, she had been right there in that veritable hell all these years.

How? How was Jasmine in trouble with Noah King? What had Andrew done?

Instructing Stavros to wait, he made a series of calls, pulling every contact he had made during his life on the streets of London.

In twenty minutes, he had the gist of the situation, and it sent his sanity reeling.

Noah King had set Jasmine's virginity up for an auction and she was texting for help.

If he hadn't spent the first fifteen years of his life in that pit, he wouldn't have believed it. The thing that burned him, though, was that she didn't ask for help. Not even now.

Instead, she'd reminded him that he owed Andrew for the countless times he had saved Dmitri from his alcoholic father's rages and then from any number of fistfights that could have killed him.

Did she think he wouldn't come unless it was to pay off a debt?

Shoving away the infernal questions, he turned to Stavros. "I...need as much cash as we can drum up instantly, upward of a hundred thousand pounds at least."

Stavros didn't even hesitate before he called their accountant. "Anything else?" he asked after he had finished.

"You're the only one I trust. If this goes sideways, I want you to...take care of Jasmine."

Stavros didn't even try to stop him, only nodded. He had taught Dmitri what it meant to do his duty.

Maybe this was his chance to start afresh. Maybe he

would have his own freedom from the guilt and emptiness that had plagued him for more than a decade once he'd set Jasmine free.

Jasmine was startled awake from a fitful sleep by the soft creaking of the door. Adrenaline deluged her and she choked down on the scream building in her chest. Slowly, she reached for the knife and sat up toward the edge of the bed. She wasn't going to leave her safety to chance.

Thankfully, the bed was in the darkest part of the room.

Noah, for all the ruthless chill in his eyes, wouldn't lay a finger on her. But John, his younger brother... She had seen that lust in his eyes every time she had run into him at the club.

She would have only one chance at striking out and she intended to take it without fail. She didn't wonder if there was a chance to escape or if Noah would rip into her for attacking his brother.

All she cared in that moment was that no one pinned her on that bed, that no one touched her.

Footsteps that were as light as her own treaded the cheap linoleum floor and she waited, crouching.

The moment the faint shadow moved, she attacked soundlessly. Her knife sliced through the air and scratched at something before she was plucked off the bed as if she was a feather.

She lashed out with her fists and legs, her screams choked by a rough hand that found her mouth effortlessly.

Her struggle lasted all of two seconds. She was grabbed and hauled against a hard body, knocking the breath out of her while a viselike arm clamped around her middle.

"Stop struggling or I will walk out and not look back."

Mindless with fear, Jasmine dug her teeth into the hard

palm, squeezing and pushing against the steel cage that clamped her.

The hold against her waist tightened, long fingers pressing into her belly and almost grazing the underside of her breasts.

But John's body wasn't honed to steel like the one holding her was, the thought pulsed through the fear. John was fleshy, round. John was... The body that held her tight was all hard muscles and sharp angles, the scent that filled her nostrils not of sweat and other body fluids but clean with a touch of water to it.

Like the ocean breeze. And only one man she knew had that intoxicating scent that had muddled her senses the last time, too.

She had been drowning in grief at Andrew's funeral, and the sight of him, all stunning and sophisticated and so different, that crisp scent of him as he had neared her had sent her on a tailspin.

"Dmitri?" she whispered, every hope, every breath hinged in that name, her pulse fluttering so fast that it whooshed in her ears.

The tightness of his hold relented, a sudden shift in the hardness that encased her. His breath landed on the rim of her ear, tickling her. "At your service, Jasmine."

Relief came at her in shuddering waves, her lungs expanding, her throat thick with pent-up fear.

Long fingers moved up and down her arms, stroking her. "Breathe, *pethi mou.*"

A streak of longing rent through her at the endearment, tearing at the hardened chunk of self-imposed loneliness that was her core. God, she hadn't been held like that in forever.

"You came," she whispered, feeling light-headed and shivery.

"Your faith in me will bloat my ego." Silky smooth and

dripping with sarcasm, his words were a whiplash against her fading willpower.

Anchoring her fingers on his forearms, she forced her spine to straighten. "From everything I hear about you," she said, her relief fading with a welcome burn of anger and grief she had nursed for the past few years, "your ego, *among other things*, is apparently already big enough."

Waves of his laughter enveloped her. His mouth opened in a smile against her jaw, sending a burst of such shocking heat through her nerves. She didn't dare turn and glance at him, for fear of combusting alive on the spot.

Why was she reacting like this to him? Was it shock?

"John's lying outside—"

She tried to jerk away from him. "God, you killed him?"

Another lethal smile flashed at her. "I promised my godfather I wouldn't waste the life he gave me."

"Nice to know you keep some of your promises."

"And then there is Stavros," he continued smoothly, ignoring her ungrateful little remark, "whose wedding is in a week, and he would not appreciate being dragged into my mess." He sighed. "So tempted as I was, I didn't kill him. I don't even use my fists anymore except to hit Stavros," he added. "And believe me, if that isn't exercising self-control, I don't know what is."

Jasmine had no idea if he was serious or joking. The fact that he had answered her request for help, even though it was what she had fervently prayed for, hit her hard now.

Was it because she hadn't expected the infamous playboy to come himself? Because she had relentlessly, *and a little obsessively*, hoped that the soft lifestyle had softened him?

Had somehow made him less?

Instead, the body that encased her felt as if it was made of steel. Realizing that she was leaning into him, she threw her elbow out.

His breath hissed out of him. "Now that we have finished our introductions, are you ready to leave this dump?"

"Dmitri…why did you attack John? Why're you here in the middle of the night?"

Darkness shadowed his face, the fluorescent light caressing his face here and there. The light gray of his eyes was the only thing she could see. And in one glimpse, they burned with such ferocity that Jasmine dropped her gaze. "I hit him because I remembered how much of a bully John was and because he was sniffing around outside your door. And I'm here at midnight because I don't trust Noah not to up the ante by morning—"

One question burned on her lips. "Did you…pay off the debt, Dmitri?"

"I didn't just pay off the debt, Jasmine. I won the—" he slipped into Greek and Jasmine had no interest in learning what the pithy word was "—*auction*. Now stop acting the damsel in distress and move, *thee mou*."

The endearment, echoing with mockery, lanced at her. "I'm not a damsel, neither am I naive enough to assume that you're a white knight."

The second her words left her, she wanted to snatch them back.

His teeth gleamed in the dark. "It heartens me to know that you know the score. I'm no white knight, neither will I risk loss of limb to save your hide."

"No?"

"No. But you already know that. What did you call me at Andrew's funeral—a self-serving bastard who doesn't know the meaning of honor or loyalty? Throwing some money at Noah to *buy* you is one thing. But my generosity doesn't stretch far enough to risk myself. So how about we postpone our chat?"

The dark of dawn cloaked them as they exited into the

street. A gasp left her as she saw the sleek Bugatti motorcycle tucked neatly out of sight.

So what the dirty rags reported about his lifestyle was true. Bugatti bikes, and a yacht and countless women—Dmitri Karegas finally had everything he had ever wanted.

And he hadn't lifted even a finger to help Andrew.

I have asked Dmitri for help and he cut me off, Jas. He's not the boy we knew once. Andrew's words resonated in her head, building a fire of hatred in her gut. But he had helped her today, the sensible part of her piped up.

"You're staring at it as if it were a viper that would strike you."

Feeling the intensity of his perusal, she shook her head.

It didn't matter what Dmitri had become. It *couldn't* matter to her.

He was an old friend who happened to have enough money to bail her out of a sticky situation. She would pay him back, even if it meant she would have to go hungry half the time, and they would be through with each other and that would be that.

"Jasmine?" Dmitri probed softly.

Cold October wind pressed against the exposed skin at her neck, sinking and seeping into her flesh. The worn-out sweatshirt she had pulled on last night offered meager protection. Her muscles shivered at the biting cold.

He chucked off his leather jacket. And held it out to her.

Her hands wrapped around herself to ward off the cold, she stared back at him.

"I don't need it…" Her teeth chattered right in the middle of her sentence. Bloody traitorous body! "I'm fine," she finished lamely.

He said nothing, his hand still stretched out toward her.

The silence between them stretched, sharply contrasted by the growing traffic around them. He pushed the helmet down onto his head. Though his face was hidden by the visor, Jasmine could feel the thread of his fury beneath it.

His very stillness in the wake of it was disconcerting and she marveled at his control.

Why? Why was he so angry with her? Why couldn't he take the damn helmet off so that she could properly look at him, so that she could at least guess his thoughts?

She must still be under shock after the past few days because somehow the latter mattered more to her than his anger.

She wanted to see those solemn gray eyes; she wanted to see that broken blade of his nose, the tender smile that had always curved his mouth just for her. The strength of how fiercely she wanted to feel those arms around her once again… It was insanity.

More than anything, she wanted to see how much he'd changed from the sixteen-year-old who had left with his wealthy godfather.

From as far back as she could remember, Dmitri had been rough, almost violent, got into every fight he could manage. Only Andrew had been able to calm him, reach him at a level that no one could.

His mother's death did that to him was all her brother would say when she probed. She remembered how fiercely Dmitri had fought against leaving with his godfather. It had taken Andrew countless hours to convince him.

But once he'd left, Dmitri hadn't looked back. Not once.

He had easily forsaken Andrew and all the promises he'd made, had become the überwealthy playboy who cared nothing for those he had left behind.

And then he'd started appearing in the gossip columns, his wild parties, expensive toys and the countless women he dated—*dated* being a euphemism—making him infamous. One time, he had even come close to marrying a Russian supermodel.

In short, his life now was spheres away from hers.

"Before you read something into this—" she sensed his sardonic smile rather than seeing it "—it's like putting a tarp on my Ferrari or a fresh coat of paint on my yacht, Jasmine. It's about protecting my possessions."

A gasp escaped her at how effortlessly cruel he was. "I still don't want it."

"Fine, freeze to your death, then."

He pushed the helmet over her head. With precise movements, he tugged the ends of the strap together tight around her chin. Jasmine jerked at the touch of his long fingers against her jaw and cheeks, a searing heat stroking her skin. The click of the strap reverberated in tune with the thud of her heart.

"I don't need—"

"I'm very possessive of all my toys."

She slapped his hand away from her chin, her rising temper drowning out the confusion. With movements as measured as she could make them, she got on the bike.

"I'm not a bloody toy that you acquired. You're just as bad as the lot of them."

Her words got cut off as the bike started with a sleek purr, pulled off like a cannon and the momentum almost threw her off the backseat.

The very real risk of flying off the bike claiming her, Jasmine held on to his shoulders, taking care to not touch him more than necessary.

A distinct sense of unease settled between her shoulder blades. What had she risked by trusting a man who had no loyalty, who thought his roots were nothing but a dirty stain that had to be removed?

CHAPTER TWO

THROUGH LITTERED STREETS and narrow alleys, Dmitri drove on and on, feeling as if the very devil was on his heels.

Usually, he felt as if he was the king of the world as the sleek machine responded to his every request, purred into a beauty of motion. Usually, he found escape from the emptiness in his gut when he drove his bike or when he took his yacht out onto the ocean.

With the wind whipping at him and the world going motionless around him, the pure throttling power of it had always calmed him.

He knew nothing of that calm now. A cascade of emotions and feelings deluged him, and it was as if he was still trying to breathe, trying to stay afloat.

It was going back to that neighborhood, he decided with a choked-back growl.

His life had been a veritable hell all those years ago and not for the reason that Stavros and Giannis assumed. Being there, he thought, would surely send him spiraling into that angry, violent teenager Giannis had suddenly found on his hands.

And it had.

That same anger and fear and shame had instantly corralled him the moment he had seen the familiarly grungy warehouse, smelled the nearby leather factory. The suffocating stench of his failure clung to his pores.

Like an invisible rope had loosened the tether he kept

on the memories he locked away, like his skin could flinch and smart again from scars that had healed on the surface long ago.

He hadn't felt this out of control since…since the night his mother had died. The road curved dangerously ahead and he throttled the gear, curving into it.

A tentative hand pressed into his shoulder, his name a soft whisper on the periphery of his roiling emotions. Jasmine's slender body slammed into him from behind, her arms vining around his midriff like clinging ropes. Her mouth was near his ear and her terrified voice broke through the black shroud of past.

"Dmitri, *please*…slow down."

Her soft entreaty finally punctured through him and he slowed.

Her hands wound around his waist snugly. She was plastered to his back from cheek to chest, and a sigh left her mouth. He clutched her hand at his waist and she pressed back silently. He didn't know who sought comfort from whom, but there was something about her embrace that calmed the turmoil inside him.

That life was over, he reminded himself. Andrew was far beyond his help. His mother was far beyond his help.

He had nothing to recommend about himself to a woman, but he had oodles of money. And with it, he would ensure Jasmine never went back to that world, would set her up for the rest of her life and walk away.

They stopped finally after an hour, dawn streaking the sky a faint pink. Her muscles cramping at sitting so still and erect on the bike, Jasmine got off the bike shakily, her legs barely holding her up.

From a dingy, neon-lit back alley to the sophisticated elegance of The Chatsfield, London, it was as if she had fallen through a tear in the fabric of the city.

Chauffeured luxury vehicles rounded the courtyard even at this time, designer-clad men and women making their way to the entrance.

Her neck craned back, she took in the majestic building and then looked down at herself. Dressed in washed-out jeans and a thin, baggy sweater, she felt like a mangy dog that the liveried bellboy would shoo away any second.

With a masculine elegance, Dmitri got off the bike and handed the keys to an eagerly waiting, uniformed valet. He came to stand next to her and instantly, a storm of butterflies unleashed in her belly.

Heat crept up her chest as she remembered the restrained power in his leanly coiled body.

After years of dreaming about getting out of that life, the reality of it happening had hit her hard. Driven by a growing sense of freedom and fear at how fast he had been going, she had wrapped herself around him. She had only sought comfort in a distressing moment, and yet now it felt shameless and weak, smacking of a familiarity that she didn't want him to think she presumed.

He hadn't pushed her off the bike, so that had to count for something.

The frigid air that met her nostrils was coated with the scent of him, and somehow became the familiar anchor in a sea of strangeness.

"You should have told me where we were going," she said, aware of the belligerence in her tone and not able to stop it.

She hated feeling as if she didn't belong. And the sad truth of her life was that she belonged in that dingy alley rather than here. She belonged more in that club that catered to the most basic sins than in this posh elegance, with men like Noah and John rather than the man Dmitri had become.

He took her elbow and pulled her forward. "You don't sound happy to be out of there."

Keeping her gaze ahead, which was sure going to break her neck, she quipped, "More like not happy to be out here. I don't want to go in there, Dmitri. I just need a few more minutes of your—"

"We're going to need a lot more than a few minutes to sort things out, Jasmine. And if I can belong here," he threw at her arrogantly, "then you can."

"Sort out...what? Why?"

His long fingers dug into her flesh as if to jostle her. She pulled at his grip with her fingers but he didn't relent. "You will not look at me. Why?"

She angled her head and caught a quick glimpse just to defy him.

Piercing gray eyes held hers in an open challenge and she turned away.

The doorman held out the door for them, a familiar smile on his face. Dmitri greeted him by name and Jasmine followed slowly. He had been so close all these years. And she had never known.

"You stay here regularly?"

"Yes."

"I didn't realize you visited London anymore."

"And you would know because you have kept in touch?" An impression of contained energy and a barely civil smile hit her. "Stavros prefers to look after the Athens side of the business."

Entering the brilliantly lit lobby from the dark, hushed luxury of the outside was like stepping into a different world. Jasmine blinked and stared around, losing her bearings for a few minutes.

Black-and-white art deco flooring complemented soft beige walls while a stunning, magnificent chandelier took center stage in the vast space. Bold lines and sweeping curves made the hotel look timelessly elegant.

And Dmitri stood in the center of it all.

Black jeans and black leather jacket made him look effortlessly breathtaking, the long, lean lines of his body drawing looks from more than one woman even in the predawn hours.

He might have started where she did, but there was an aura of casual power and panache that made Dmitri not just blend, but stand out amidst the extravagant grandeur of the hotel.

At five-ten, she matched his six-three stride easily. She only wished she could say the same of her clothes and more important, her insides. The vast foyer felt as if it would take forever to cross and all she wanted to do was to fade away from the brilliant lights.

It was not that she thought herself plain. On the contrary, she had heard all her life, and felt nauseous, that she was exotic, lush, possessed of perfect voluptuousness for her vocation. She was stared at six nights of the week and earned her living making love to a pole, but it was how she felt next to the casual elegance of the man next to her that bothered her.

The shame that always clung to her, as if it was etched into her very skin, was amplified when she stood next to him. Just as it stung her that he had seen her at such a weak moment.

As if suddenly he was a measure of her looks, her world, her very life.

She flinched when he pulled her away from the reception area toward the bank of elevators. He held her loosely and yet a thread of his emotions, not so contained, brimmed within him.

Beneath that polite smile, she had a feeling he was ragingly furious. And she was afraid of finding out why.

"The hotel is fit for a king," she said, trying to keep the utter awe she felt out of her words.

"I have a feeling that you're the opposite of impressed."

The doors of the lift closed with a soft *ping*, trapping them inside. Her heart beat like the thundering hooves of a horse when he hit the stop button.

"You have to look at me now, Jasmine" came his soft command.

"You're making a big deal out of..."

"Are you afraid of me, *thee mou*?"

Shaking her head, she looked up.

The four walls of the lift were glittering mirrors that showed her a stunningly gorgeous face.

Her femininity, beaten down and stuffed into a bag, roared a primal scream of joy at the sight of the magnificent man in front of her. Every inch of her—from her skin to her breasts, from her cells to her core—stood to attention.

His legs crossed at the ankles, his hands gripping the wall behind him, he filled the space with his masculinity. Something else burst into life in that enclosed space, swelling and arching, until Jasmine felt as though there was a hum inside her every nerve.

Even at sixteen, he had had arresting features, but now...the power he exuded and his command of the world filled the planes and angles of his face, making him a lethal combination of stunning looks and effortless masculinity.

Long, curly lashes kissed cheekbones that were honed so sharp that it was like looking at the work of a master sculptor. Deep-set gray eyes studied her just as hungrily as she studied him. As if he knew her volatile reaction to his nearness.

Of course he knew, Jasmine scolded herself. There couldn't be a man alive who looked like Dmitri and didn't know it, didn't wield it to his advantage. And the fact that she, too, with all the rules she had set in place to be able to face herself in the mirror, was staring at him with googly eyes, measuring herself against him… That woke up Jasmine like nothing else could.

Now she understood the sense of danger that had skittered through her very blood when he had held her from behind so intimately.

The danger to her didn't come from him. The danger to her came from her reaction to him.

CHAPTER THREE

DECIDING THAT HE would protect her at any cost was one thing, Dmitri thought as Jasmine devoured him with those wide eyes.

The actual logistics of what he would do with this wild creature were quite another. With lush breasts and narrow hips that swayed with every step she took, from the way she tucked that tumbling jet-black hair behind her ear to the pouty mouth that came from no injection, Jasmine was not simply beautiful, but stunningly sexy.

Was that the reason for that ridiculous auction? Had some man coveted her because of those Arab genes that she had inherited from an absentee father, and Noah had turned it to his advantage? What horrific scheme had she caught herself in?

Round jet-black eyes, dark arched eyebrows that suited perfectly those big eyes, a sharp, bladelike nose and a pointed chin.

There was not an ounce of extra flesh on her face, giving her a lean, sharp look. As if every bone in that face had been sculpted by years of hunger and sleepless nights. Her hair, jet-black and thickly curling, was pulled back tightly, exaggerating the feral sharpness of her features. One curl dangled alongside a sharply defined jawline.

There was an alert look in her eyes even now, just as there had been in that warehouse. The straight, tense line of her shoulders, her sharp breaths... He realized how alien this was to her.

How alien he was to her...

When he had seen her five years ago, she had barely turned eighteen, and had looked nothing like this...except for that wary distrust.

It had been there then, too. But where she had barely glanced at him then, her bold gaze drank him in today.

He had never experienced such a thorough, artless appraisal. Women came on to him all the time and he enjoyed it, but Jasmine's searing gaze was more than basic female curiosity.

It was as though she was looking for something, or someone. And instead of that shallow echo he was so used to, he felt something inside him vibrate in response to her look.

As if a part of him that had lain dormant and unfeeling for so long suddenly uncoiled itself at the sight of her. Dangerously tempting and thoroughly unwise... He wondered how to distance himself from it.

Because as hungry as he'd been to feel something like that, he had nothing to give her.

"No one would know you were from the streets," she said with a brittleness that he wouldn't have associated with her.

"And why do you sound as if that's the worst thing in the world, Jasmine?" He would not call her Jas even though it fluttered on his tongue. Which was strange, because how could a woman's name have so much power over him? "It's a pit of desperation and addiction and violence. Why should I ever want to look as if I belonged there once? Why should anyone who had a chance to get out of there still cling to it?" Steel resonated in his voice at the end there but he couldn't help it.

Her eyelashes fluttered, and he had a feeling she was

trying to calm herself down. She failed. When she looked at him, she fairly bristled with aggressiveness. "Of course not. And God forbid anything stand in the way of you leaving the past behind, Dmitri, anything even remotely dirty and poor taint your extravagant lifestyle now."

He pushed off the wall, furious energy burning through his veins. Instantly, she flattened herself against the wall. And the startled look in her eyes more than anything calmed him down.

Let her think what she wants, he told himself.

He had never cared what the world thought of him. Why would he care about what Jasmine said? But he couldn't allow her to taunt him like that; he couldn't allow her to think even for a second that she knew him.

He turned all the energy in him into cutting scorn, delivering it in a silky-smooth tone. "Before you castigate me for wanting out of that life, let's not forget how this night started, *thee mou*. Let's not forget whose money and power saved whose ass in this story, *ne*?"

"Maybe you believe your life is not valuable enough to get out of there, but I will not feel guilty for thinking mine is. Nor will I feel guilty about enjoying the fruits of my hard labor. Giannis might have—"

"Pulled you out of the hellhole that was our life, but I know that it was you and your friend…"

"Stavros Sporades," he added.

"That it was you two that put his textile company on the global map, especially when everything else is folding in this economy," she added, as if she was offering him recompense for angering him. "I have followed your—" he had a feeling she wouldn't say the actual word that she wanted to "—success the past few years."

And suddenly, it was as though a hard fist jammed into his throat. She had known he was rich, then. She had known that he could have helped. Even as she refused to admit it, she had known, all along, that he would come if she asked.

And yet, she had waited so long… Which night would have made it too long?

Fury, reminding him of broken bones and painful fists, flew hot through him. "Have you? Gratifying to know that I held your interest for so many years, *pethi mou*. And a little shocking that you have somehow lost the good sense I thought you possessed."

The lift opened just then and he walked out without checking to see if she followed.

By the time she walked past the dramatic reception hall into the sitting lounge of the suite, Jasmine felt numb to the extravagance of her surroundings.

It was a toss-up between the electricity that burned between Dmitri and her and the reach of his wealth and sphere.

A finely carved wood and marble fireplace dominated the lounge, which was decorated with black leather furniture.

Her running shoes sank into the thick carpet with a soft hiss.

Jasmine had barely caught her breath when a woman walked into the lounge. Her hair was mussed around her fragile, sleep-ruffled face, her long legs bared in shorts.

"Dmitri?" she whispered, her shocked glance taking in the both of them. "You took so long…"

"Leah? What are you doing here?" The concern in Dmitri's voice was as unmistakable as the lacerating sarcasm when he addressed Jasmine.

Suddenly, being a spectator to a romantic reunion between Dmitri and his latest girlfriend was the last thing Jasmine wanted to be.

The woman crossed the last few steps, genuine worry

etched on her brow. Dmitri enfolded her so gently that it sent a pang through Jasmine. "When you were taking so long, he dropped me off here. He's been calling every fifteen minutes…" Her gasp pierced through Jasmine.

"Dmitri, you're bleeding." With that, Leah clicked her cell phone on and left the room.

The sharp hiss of his exhale, the way he had held himself so rigidly on the bike… Her gut heaving, Jasmine turned him around roughly and lifted his leather jacket.

A patch of red stained the tear on his pristine white shirt around his abdomen, a stark contrast against the rest of it.

Jasmine stared at the dried blood and the way the shirt clung to his skin. Bile filled her throat as the metallic scent washed over her. Shivers set forth from the base of her spine. As if her attacking Dmitri when he had come to save her was the last straw…

Pressing her hand to her forehead, she tried to breathe past the rawness in her throat. "I could have killed you… I thought John would sneak in in the middle of the night and I was just being cautious… I never…"

"I did not ask why you attacked me," he said in that monotone voice again. He sounded angrier at her being upset than that she had wounded him. "*Theos*, I don't care that you tried to protect yourself. I care that you have led a life that requires that you sleep with a knife under your pillow."

She flinched at the disgust in his words.

For as long as she had known, men had only looked at her cheaply, with lust glimmering in their eyes. And once she had started working her current job four years ago, it had only gotten worse, shame and self-disgust her only companions.

So why the hell did she care what Dmitri thought of her?

His hand under her chin, he lifted it up. She clutched her eyes closed to lock away the tears. The depth of her reaction to him, his words scared her.

"Look at me, Jasmine." Something rumbled in that soft command. She would have called it desperation if she thought she could hold together one sane thought at the moment.

His hands moved up and down her arms as if he was calming down a spooked animal. "You're shaking again. *Theos*, stop being afraid of me."

"I'm not afraid of you," she whispered, opening her eyes. Dark stubble surrounded that carved mouth. "I'm so sorry, Dmitri…"

He shook his head. "You grazed me really good with the serrated edge but it's only a flesh wound."

She ran a shaking finger over the mended bridge of his shattered nose, a tendril of desperate emotion engulfing her.

"I don't remember ever being so terrified as that night when John punched you," she said, remembering the horrific night when John had broken Dmitri's nose. "I thought you would kill him."

A haunting memory flashed through those deceptively calm eyes. "If not for Andrew, I would have." A smile cut his mouth then, transforming his face again. It was like seeing someone intensely familiar slip on a mask and become a stranger. "For a woman who defends that filthy world, you're acting strange at the sight of a little blood."

Her finger moved down his nose, hovered over his mouth, her heart thundering in her chest.

"Jas…" Her name was a raw warning on his lips.

An immense stillness seemed to come over him, the faintest of shudders moving his narrow seamed mouth. His fingers clasped her wrist tight, as if he was truly afraid of her touching his mouth. "You're still in shock."

Was he convincing her or himself? she wondered. She had seen her mum waste herself away in a bottle of rum, had seen Andrew breathe his last... Grief and fear for her life had all been consuming her since Noah's men had arrived at her doorstep three days ago, and yet it was this moment that threatened to shove her heart out of her chest...

This craven yearning to touch him, to discover if there was anything left of the boy who had treated her as if she was the most precious thing he had ever held... It was madness.

Because he had left that boy behind a long time ago when he had walked out with his godfather. Leaving Andrew and her behind.

Far, far behind.

"Dmitri?" a man's deep voice called.

It jolted her out of her feverlike delirium and Jasmine tried to collect her breath.

"It might be a flesh wound, but you should still have it sterilized and cleaned up," the man continued. "It doesn't look as though Jasmine uses that knife for chopping vegetables."

She looked up to find Dmitri looking at her with a sardonic gleam in his eyes, his brows raised in question.

He held her wrist aloft and returned it to her side. Then he gently nudged her back. To his friend, he added, "Hand me the first-aid kit, Stavros."

Enough, Jas!

Was she so desperate for a connection from their awful past, so lonely that even Dmitri's begrudging help would do?

She was damned, however, if she let his posh friends walk all over her, or insult her dirty roots.

Stavros, whose face was a study in austerity and cold arrogance, gazed at her, his expression inscrutable.

"I assure you, Mr. Sporades, my knife is not as filthy as you imagine."

A smile touched the man's mouth but his expression didn't lose the severity. "You mistake me, Jasmine," he said, assuming a familiarity that shocked her. "I'm in awe of how cunningly you found a way out of your predicament. Although I—"

"He wishes, *rightly*—" Dmitri cut in, frost turning his eyes into a thundering gray "—that you had not put yourself in such a dangerous situation in the first place."

"Put myself in that situation? You talk as if this was a game to me. You think I...I wanted to *sell* myself like that?"

Such a savage growl erupted from Dmitri that it was like seeing a cat transform into a tiger, vicious claws unsheathed. "You don't want to know how I dare ask that question, *yineka mou*, not in front of company. That is a discussion you and I will have later, when I'm not in danger of strangling you for the company you keep."

The silence that followed the softly spoken threat was deafening, the shock on his friends' faces sending a ripple down Jasmine's spine.

Jasmine felt as if she had been slapped, as if her shame was written all over her face. There was none of that easy humor, that uncaring attitude that he had worn in the past couple of hours. "I've had enough of you and your insulting—"

She had barely turned around when his broad frame, bursting with contained violence, blocked her. "Do not test my patience, Jasmine."

Something in the glint of his eye warned Jasmine to shut up.

"How bad is that cut?" Stavros intervened as if the room wasn't crackling with furious energy.

"I can attend to it myself." Dmitri turned and grinned,

a wicked glint in his eyes. The transformation from brooding violence to charming rogue was so swift that Jasmine did a double take. "Or Leah can attend to me."

Jasmine had never seen him smile like that.

Innocence had never been a luxury they had been afforded, and for as long back as she could remember of her childhood, Dmitri had been in it. And not this smiling, outrageous playboy who looked as though nothing touched him...

The expression in his eyes was dazzling, wicked and not...completely real. He knew what his outrageous remark would do and he had used it to deflect attention from him and his wound.

That smile was a practiced facade, she thought with a frown.

Leah shook her head. "Dmitri, stop taunting him. And, Stavros, really, enough with the caveman—"

"Tell your husband that I'm not sixteen anymore and he doesn't need to patch me up." This was Dmitri again, winking wickedly at Leah. "I had hoped you would have cured him of all this duty nonsense in your bed, *pethi mou.*"

A curse flew from the deceptively calm Stavros.

"You're his wife?" Jasmine said to the blushing Leah, realizing she had spoken out loud when Dmitri looked at her.

"Who did you think she was?"

Challenge. Dare. Belligerence. All of it wrapped in a smooth tone.

With three sets of eyes resting on her, Jasmine flushed but refused to let him embarrass her. She poured defiance into her tone. "Your current squeeze.

"I'm sorry." She said this to Leah, who was shaking her head at both men.

"Don't be." Leah smiled. "Dmitri is being his usual

beastly self. I'm Leah Sporades. Giannis, their godfather, was my grandfather."

Jasmine stood awkwardly as Stavros and Leah argued with Dmitri with an obvious familiarity while he threw outrageous remarks at them.

I knew him before you did.

The errant thought dropped into her head and she sent a startled glance toward Dmitri.

His gaze stayed on her, intense and brooding, as if he would like nothing but to skin her alive with his words. Seconds piled on as that same awareness locked them in their own little world. What would happen when his friends left?

Running a hand over her forehead, she looked away. The faster she got out of here the better.

She grabbed the kit from the unsuspecting Stavros and turned to Dmitri. "Stop with the macho posturing and sit down. The cut is on the far left side and you're left-handed."

His grin vanishing, Dmitri looked at her as if she had suddenly sprouted two heads.

She sighed. That mutinous, wary expression in his eyes... *That* she remembered.

"Strip, Dmitri."

"Usually I'm filled with uncontainable anticipation at that command from a woman," he said with an exaggerated leer, "but give back the kit to Stavros, Jasmine."

Unbuttoning his shirt, Dmitri pulled it off his wound. Only a jerk of his mouth betrayed his pain. Ridges of leanly sculpted muscles defined his broad chest, only a smattering of dark hair dotting the olive-toned skin.

Her cheeks instantly tightened, her mouth dry as Jasmine tried to not stare. She took a step toward him, determined to act normal. "I'll make it fast."

Dmitri glared at her. "I'd rather you not touch me at all."

"Why not? I've sewed up so many of Andrew's wounds growing up that I—"

"Like Stavros pointed out so well, we don't know where *you and your hands* have been. And yes, you are super-tough to have made it all on your own for so many years... But we both know that you are a little fragile right now, *ne*? You were crawling all over me on the bike and—"

"Because you were driving like a maniac," she yelled, her face heating up.

"—and a minute ago, you got upset at the sight of the small gash. I'd rather you not look at me with those sad, puppy eyes while you tend to me as if this was some grand reunion that we both have been breathlessly waiting for for years. My generosity toward you is fast disappearing and the cut burns like hell."

The kit fell from her fingers, thudding like a drum in the silence.

There were so many offensive things in there that for a second, she couldn't even sift through them all. Only stood weightless while the cruelty in his words carved through her.

Then the slow, merciful burn of humiliation spread across her throat and cheeks, merciful because anything was better than that hollow ache, her ribs squeezing her lungs tighter and tighter.

His words should not have touched her. He was nothing to her. She had hated him for years on principle. And yet his words knocked the breath out of her.

Was it because she had never been so *literally* saved from a situation before? Because, for most of her life, she had only depended on herself, and seeing a man like Dmitri come to her aid was warping her sense of reality?

Or was she just like her mum after all? One kind word from a man and she was ready to fall over herself and into his arms?

She struggled to hold his gaze but she did, pouring all the hatred, *for him and for herself*, into that look.

"You're right. I'm not myself..." She drew in a shuddering breath. "And you... You're not..."

His face was a tight mask over his angular features, his eyes suddenly hauntingly vulnerable. "Do not assume to know me, Jasmine."

She shook her head, feeling immensely weary. "No, I don't, do I? Have your cut looked at or let it fester and rot you, for all I care. I need a little more of your precious time and then I want out of here."

Holding her shoulders rigidly, she turned.

The sympathy in Leah's eyes was much too real, and Jasmine steeled herself against it. Stumbling through the lounge, she ducked into the first room and closed the door behind her and then walked into the en-suite bathroom.

A sea of white marble greeted her. With a tub long and wide enough for her to swim in, with gleaming gold taps, cold porcelain tiles and thick, fluffy towels, it was her version of paradise.

Tempted as she was to soak in the bath, she stripped and headed for the shower, needing to wash off the fear and grime of the past two days. If only she could so easily wash off the stink of her life...

The moment the water hit her, something in her unraveled. With a deep breath, Jasmine let the tears that had been threatening all night, out.

Only once, Jas, she warned herself.

She would cry just this once, without caring what it meant. She would let herself be weak just this one time. And then she would walk out and not look back.

She had been right in rejecting his offer of money when Andrew had died.

With the hatred of a thousand suns, she promised herself she would never set eyes on Dmitri Karegas again after tonight.

CHAPTER FOUR

DMITRI HISSED OUT a sharp breath as Stavros dabbed his wound with an alcohol wipe. Yet the burn of it over the open flesh was nothing compared to the burn in his gut.

The image of Jas's face, her mouth trembling, her wide eyes stricken with hurt, would haunt him for the rest of his life. Along with a hundred other images of her.

Jas, looking at him with a toothless smile, Jas, at nine, sitting by him in companionable silence while he nursed a broken nose, Jas, her tears overflowing onto her cheeks as he said goodbye to her and Andrew...

Jas, as she glared at him with bristling hatred and fury at Andrew's funeral five years ago...

And now this Jas, who saw through his veneer to the real him, who had melted into his arms with such vulnerability in her eyes...

Who had looked at him as if he was everything...

A furious cascade of such hunger churned in his gut that he had to grasp the handrest to anchor himself. Just the torrent of emotions that had deluged him ever since she had come at him with that knife was proof enough.

No! That look had been nothing but a result of shock.

He didn't want her to look at him like that, as if he was her hero and knight wrapped in one.

He was no one's hero, and definitely not hers. He shattered women's silly romantic notions of him on a regular basis.

Yet the hurt in her eyes disturbed him far more than it should have.

Theos, where was the woman who had so thoroughly despised him that day?

Setting Jasmine's expectations regarding him shouldn't require this much thought and second-guessing.

"You know," Leah's voice cut in, "I always thought you were the kinder one between Stavros and you." She sighed. "I'll wait in the limo, Stavros. I don't want to embarrass Jasmine anymore but if possible, please convince her to come with us."

"She won't accept anyone's charity," Dmitri said, before he could curb the words. Because he had tried once and she had bristled as if he had made an indecent proposition.

Leah's displeasure swelled in the silence even after she left.

Unrolling gauze, Stavros leveled him a flat look. Dmitri refused to take the bait.

Stavros cut up a strip of medicinal gauze and covered up the wound and then neatly put on a plaster. Then he shut the plastic case and tucked it away. Uncoiling to his height, he finally met Dmitri's gaze. "She seems...very innocent, Dmitri."

He understood the awe in Stavros's voice. Dmitri had been prepared for the shock of seeing Jasmine after all these years, but she was nothing like he had imagined.

From the moment he had entered that house, a tight fist had formed in his gut and it showed no signs of loosening. To find her like he did today, to imagine what would have happened if he had been late... Everything inside him ignited into a mindless fury, every lesson he had learned in controlling his temper consumed by that fear.

"Something I didn't have when Giannis plucked me from there, you mean?" he challenged Stavros.

"Yes."

Stavros's unsaid question reverberated in that single word, but Dmitri was in no mood to talk about the lack of his innocence. Stavros had come to mean more to him than even his godfather but he wouldn't go into his past even for him.

He refused to let it leave a mark on him.

"You don't know to handle her," Stavros said in that arrogant tone of his that drove Leah crazy.

"You're afraid I'm going to corrupt that innocence," Dmitri stated flatly.

Jasmine was like the key to the Pandora's box he had left behind a long time ago. And all he wanted with the key was to throw it away and not look back.

"No," Stavros replied, surprising him. "But it is also obvious that she—"

"She's a debt, Stavros, and I pay them."

A lethal smile touched his friend's mouth. "Tell me your plans for her."

He remained silent, drawing a complete blank.

What was he supposed to do with her now? She had no place in his life, even a minuscule one.

"We both know that you can't just let her walk out of here. Not without ensuring she's not going to be a danger to herself."

"Danger she's courted recklessly." The words rattled out of Dmitri on a wave of anger.

Why the hell hadn't she come to him before this? *Theos*, he understood addictions and the damage they caused, but for Andrew to leave her with so much debt, a debt that Dmitri had no doubt was the result of his gambling…?

Fury and powerlessness flew in his veins because Andrew wasn't even here anymore for Dmitri to take it out on.

"So she deserves to be left to her fate?" Stavros asked

with rising incredulity. "Is this how you would've helped if Calista had been in trouble?"

"*Christos*, she's not going to…" The horror of the night when Stavros's sister had died cut him off.

But then, none of them had known Calista had been on such a self-destructive path until it had been years too late. Pain pounded through his veins at the thought of Jasmine going down that path. Look at the situation she had found herself in. "She's not going to calmly accept whatever I propose."

"I know you hate responsibility of any kind, Dmitri, but this is—"

"*Theos*, Stavros, she does not belong with me. Not for a moment, much less for days."

Stavros looked at him again, something emerging in his gaze. As if he could sense the panic in Dmitri's words. As if he could see the noose tightening around Dmitri's throat. "Then, you should have never answered her call for help.

"What about her is bothering you so much, Dmitri? I have never seen you in such a…*state* when it comes to a woman. You change them on a weekly basis. Why is she different?"

Dmitri pushed a hand through his hair, feeling as though his life was slipping out of his hands. How he wished he could fob her off on Stavros…

"You don't want to be responsible for her and yet your conscience won't let her walk away. How about you do not anger her, then?"

"Where was this infinite wisdom when it was Leah we were dealing with?" he couldn't help pointing out.

"Learn from my lesson, then, won't you?" Stavros growled, steel edging into his tone. As it always did when even the mention of how close he had come to losing Leah came up. "If you hurt her again, the damage she does to you might not be so minimal. Or even worse, she could just turn around and go back to that same world."

"Her feelings are not my concern." That was it. Jasmine could rant and rage at him all she wanted. All he cared about was that the woman was alive. If he had to shred her to pieces to do it, he would, again and again. But he wouldn't let her return to that life.

He had failed so many people in his life, but he couldn't fail Jasmine.

Jasmine stepped into the elegantly decorated bedroom and flopped onto the bed. The robe she had put on slid silkily against her skin but she just couldn't get herself to wear the same jeans and sweater again. Not until she got them washed, at least.

Only silence came from the front lounge. Her heart thudding loudly, she looked up.

Dmitri prowled into the room and leaned against the wall, the movement pulling one lapel of his unbuttoned shirt higher, exposing a rope of leanly sculpted muscle. A gauze pad near his abdomen stood out white against his olive skin.

One of his brows lifted, a sardonic smile twisting his mouth.

Sinuous heat bloomed low in her belly, the sight of his naked torso a temptation like she had never imagined.

The luxurious black satin scrunched in her fingers painted a picture of her writhing beneath that leanly coiled frame, all of that simmering intensity unleashed on her, while he worshipped her with the mouth that had pierced her so much…

"Jasmine?"

His frown prompted her out of her fantasies, her skin heating up.

She was used to attention of the most extreme kind,

knew lust in all its forms. And yet, when Dmitri looked at her, even innocently as he was doing now, as if he could see into her head and soul, she was extremely aware of it.

Of all the men in the world, something inside her reacted with a violent energy to Dmitri. Maybe it was because she had known him as a kid. Maybe because, for the first time in years, she was with a man and she didn't have to worry about whether he was motivated by lust or some other inferior motive.

That was it.

Dmitri, for all his crushing words, was safe.

For years, she had wondered if the life she had adapted to to survive had somehow corrupted her ability to feel this kind of need, if her body would ever feel like it was anything but an instrument she had honed to make a living…if she would feel free enough…wondered if there was anything pure left in her thoughts except for the technicality of it…

Yet that it was Dmitri that incited her like this… It left her shaking to her very bones.

Didn't her body know that she was supposed to hate him even if he looked like a Greek god? That he was a man who turned his back on friends because they didn't fit into his new life?

She was like a deer planning her escape route, Dmitri decided, leaning against the door. Not that he didn't think it was for the best.

The moment he saw her on the bed, *his bed*, in his robe, even if it fell to her ankles, his blood had vanished south.

She had looked so lovely for a second there, claws withdrawn. Like a lioness who wanted to be petted for a little while. Before she most likely ate you.

"You look as if you have a fever."

She nodded. "I don't feel… I'm just achy all over."

Her words emerged as a rough croak. The soft admission from her was as strange as the feverish look in those dark black eyes. Scrubbed of sleep and any lingering softness that he had ruthlessly pushed away, they glowed with determination. And regret punched him in the gut even as he knew that it was better this way.

He didn't want her all soft and melting. He wanted her to fight him and hate him.

Had she been hurt in their tussle? he thought then, the very idea horrifying him. Frowning, he took a step forward and clasped her cheek.

She flinched away from him. A silent roar burst into life inside of him, and he forced himself to take multiple breaths.

Theos, he hated when she flinched at his nearness like that…

Which was a thousand kinds of insanity because he had practically yelled at her to not come near him.

Stavros had taught him well. It took all of his willpower to control that wild thing inside him that wanted her hands on him. All of her on him. Reminded himself that all he offered a woman was sex. And Jasmine deserved a lot more.

Clenching his jaw, he fought for composure. "Did I hurt you when I tackled you?"

"No. I just… I pulled a muscle the other day and it's still bothering me."

"Let me see it."

"No." Jasmine drew in a deep breath and forced the words to come out evenly. "Thanks for coming so promptly today, Dmitri. For literally coming to my rescue."

"You almost choked on that, *ne*?"

She shrugged, refusing to take the bait.

He entered the bedroom and went to the wardrobe.

Panic blooming in her gut, she looked around the bedroom she had run into.

It was his bedroom, of course.

She tried to slide off the silky sheets. And lost the little dignity she had in the process when he turned around, his brows raised.

Sleeping in Dmitri's bed was the last thing she needed. It was far too intimate for the little peace that she needed for her overactive mind.

She dangled her legs on the side of the bed. "I didn't realize this was your bedroom. I will just…"

"Stay," he ordered her softly.

With his back still against the wardrobe, he extracted a perfectly pressed white cotton shirt with sure precision, shrugged off the bloodied shirt. Too mesmerized by the sight of his corded biceps and chest to even pretend otherwise, Jasmine watched as he pulled on the fresh shirt.

"I will sleep in the longue or order housekeeping to clean up Stavros's room." He buttoned it down, his gaze taking in her flushed face with a casual indifference. "Are you hungry?"

Getting up and padding away from the bed, she walked to the chaise longue. "No. And you don't have to babysit me. I just want to crash for a few hours."

"I have no interest in spending the night babysitting you. Tell me…how did Noah agree to this outrageous idea of an auction?"

"You know how."

Another step closer. But caught between the bed and him, there was no way to escape. Retribution that he had threatened shone in every line of his body. "Dmitri…"

"Enlighten me again how it happened."

"Even after all these years, we still owed him money. Noah would have liked for me to sign away my entire life and I didn't want to continue—" a shudder went through her spine "—there anymore. I thought of you and suggested he put me up for auction."

He stared down at her as if he could see through her skin and into the very heart of her. "Where was he going to find buyers if not for me?"

Something in his question struck a chord of fear in Jasmine. "There weren't any others."

"Noah is not famous for his kindness. I don't understand how he agreed to your condition."

"Because all the world knows that you're a gazillionaire and Noah just happens to know that at one time you used to have a conscience. I gave him an opening to exploit that. If you're through being disgusted with me—"

"Disgusted? *Theos*, what the hell was Andrew thinking to leave you with so much debt? Why didn't he—"

Just hearing her brother judged for what little he could have done inflamed her. "Don't speak his name."

"He should have taken better care of you. I don't understand—"

Shivering from head to toe, she struggled to keep the grief at bay. Even after five years, it shredded her strength and composure with its claws. "How do you know what he did or didn't do? You left us."

Was that it? Had she hated him all these years because he had left her alone with an alcoholic mother and a brother addicted to gambling away the very little they had ever had? Was her bitter envy over his better life at the root of it all?

"I didn't have a choice, Jasmine."

"You didn't have a choice except to forget us? He always watched your back, stopped you from getting yourself killed. If not for him, you would have died a violent death a long time ago."

Every inch of his face became immobile under her attack. He stood absolutely still, calmly absorbing her insults.

Only the haunting depths of his eyes betrayed his shock. "You think I need a reminder, *Theos mou*, that without Andrew, there would have been nothing left of me for Giannis to save..."

God, what the hell had she said?

The cynical curve of his mouth... The emptiness in his eyes... She never wanted to be witness to that ever again.

She didn't want to see that flash of pain in his eyes ever again, much less cause it.

"That...that came out wrong. I just... I don't know what's wrong with me. I've never..." She took a bracing breath. "Seeing you just reminds me that he's forever gone, Dmitri. That he never had a single chance to break away from it all."

He stepped away from her as if to avoid the poison of her words. "Until I can ensure that there's no danger to you, you have no choice but to face me, Jasmine." Still, he didn't sound angry or upset. Still, he only spoke about her safety.

As if it was an onerous duty he had to take on even if she was ungrateful.

Jasmine wanted to kick herself for her impulsive mouth. Or curl into a ball and cry. In one swoop, she had spewed out all the bitterness she had struggled to keep at bay for years. She couldn't bear to look at herself, much less at Dmitri. She couldn't bear to be in his presence for a second longer without wanting to slap herself.

It was being near him, she realized. From the moment he had stepped in there, it was as if she had lost all sense of herself. It was as if she had forgotten all the hard lessons she had learned so early in life.

"I have seven thousand and change saved that I can pay you instantly. The rest of it will take me time, but I will pay you back even if I have to..."

A slow grin spread across his devilish mouth. He

shifted his feet, bit his lower lip, as if to contain the laughter spilling out, leaned his hip against the wall as if he were posing for a photo shoot and smiled again. The veins in his forearms stood out as he folded his arms, oozing sex appeal.

Jasmine's breath caught at the sheer, stark beauty of it.

There was nothing false or practiced about the curve of his mouth now.

It lit up his light gray eyes, carved a dimple in his cheek. Her knees turned to mush as he dipped his head low and batted at her with his shoulder. "So you're determined to pay me back, then, *yes*?"

Of course, the man didn't need his fists anymore. He could charm the birds from the sky with that smile. Was it any wonder that women threw themselves at his feet? What woman wouldn't want him to look at her with need in those gorgeous eyes? What woman wouldn't want those rough hands on her, that luscious mouth driving her wild?

She was getting hot just thinking about it. "Every last penny," she croaked out.

"How?"

"I'll come up with something."

"You know, Jas…" He pressed the heels of his palms to his eyes in an exaggerated show of patience. "Spanking's never been my thing but, *Theos*, I'm *so tempted* to give it a try right now. You and your ideas and your plans…"

She gasped, heat streaking her cheeks. "I was running out of options."

He prowled toward her like a predator. Heat from his body enveloped her, coating her very breath.

"And what if someone else ended up buying…*you*?"

"You're trying to scare me."

"There was someone else, Jas, someone who was willing to pay a lot of money to own you."

Jas remained silent, fear and confusion stealing rational thought from her.

"Didn't you think of contacting me even once? Did you have to wait until it got this desperate?"

She had. She had thought of him countless times, her body and mind weary after another long night, after facing another of her mother's drunken episodes. After feeling as if she would never make a dent in her debt, after facing another man look at her as if he could own her body and soul for a few bucks. After seeing her life pass day after day in that pit.

In a moment of weakness, she had called Katrakis Textiles in Athens once. The receptionist had even politely asked her for her name. In the end, she had chickened out.

In the end, it had been easier to hate him from a distance than take his pity.

"I don't like depending on anyone for anything," she said instead.

"Fate has a way of punching us with exactly what we don't want. There was someone else who bid for you. Which meant Noah had two dogs out for the same bone, and he let us go at it."

Another bidder? Her knees gave out and she sank to the longue.

Sweat beaded her brow, nausea climbing up her throat. Noah had tricked her. If Dmitri hadn't come along, he would have sold her virginity to someone else.

The horror of what could have happened filled her with dread.

"Noah said you called it a virginity auction. And that's what it truly was. What I can't figure out is who else wanted to pay off that debt and why."

Her head spun in a thousand different directions and Jasmine struggled to hold on to her sanity. Clutching her head, she walked away from him.

Just leave. Don't care what he paid, Jas. He can afford it.

Walk away, the survivor in her begged.

"How much did you pay Noah?"

"You're not my priciest toy, if that's what worries you."

Her gut heaved with anticipated dread, her right eye twitching uncontrollably from keeping her gaze so straight. Something was very wrong; she knew it in her bones.

"Stop taunting me, Dmitri. How much do I owe you?"

"A hundred and thirty thousand pounds, but since I'm feeling generous I'll round it down to an even hundred."

A hundred thousand pounds? Her gut flopped to her feet. "That can't be true. That much money... It's ridiculous, God..."

Clutching the wall behind her, she gasped for breath. "This is my worst nightmare come true... *Oh, God*..." It would take her ten lifetimes to make so much money. She would never be able to pay him back, never walk away from this.

"Being saved from a life of trading your body is your worst nightmare?"

Uncontrollable shivers overtook her. Hunger and lack of sleep from the past two days hit her like a battering ram, the sheer willpower with which she had kept herself going, shattering finally. "No. Bound to you eternally by this debt is."

She swayed and sank to the thickly carpeted floor.

A soft curse ripped through the air before she was pulled up like a rag doll. "*Theos*, Jas." His voice wasn't loud, yet it carried something. His gaze searched her, his fingers splayed against her jaw, a strange glitter darkening his eyes. "Now is not the time to lose that reckless pride."

Pushing his hands away, she sank back onto the chaise

longue. Her body felt boneless, as if she would never stop falling.

All she wanted was to curl up and sleep for the next decade. All she wanted was to let someone else bear the burden, just once. "How am I going to pay you back? Lord, what am I going to do?" she muttered to herself.

The bedroom door opened and an army of uniformed staff set down an array of dishes that had her gut twisting with hunger. She looked at the clock, which said five in the morning.

The staff vanished just as they had appeared, with minimal fuss, making her wonder if she had imagined them.

"Until you figure out a way, you will eat, sleep and generally keep your presence in my life to a minimum."

Swallowing at the mouthwatering aroma from the dishes, she nodded. Eyed the distance from the chaise to the table and groaned.

With a curse that sounded filthy to even her untrained ears, he stopped by the table and lifted a silver dome off a plate. "When did you eat last?"

"A cheeseburger about twenty hours ago," she whispered pathetically.

Pushing her legs out of his way none too gently, and careful enough to not even accidentally touch her hip that was propped up, he sat down at the foot of the chaise. Forking pasta with his left hand, which was such a familiarly intimate gesture from her childhood that a lump formed in her throat, he brought it to her mouth.

Jasmine closed her mouth over the farfalle eagerly.

"Don't make a habit of this, Jas."

He sounded uncomfortable, wary. Was he afraid that she would climb all over him again and embarrass them both?

Closing her eyes, Jas chewed, relishing the thick white sauce. "Won't even remember this, Dmitri."

She ate in silence while the influx of carbs lulled her

to sleep. She finished off a bottle of water and stretched back down on the chaise.

"I'll see you later."

She lifted her thumbs as he stilled by the door, pensive. She felt like that mangy dog again. Only instead of letting the doorman kick her, Dmitri had decided to keep her.

Something strange was going on with him. The fleeting thought came to her even as her head felt as if it was filled with cotton candy.

One minute, he was shredding her into pieces with such ruthlessness, and the next…such tenderness showed in his eyes that she thought she would shatter in the face of it.

"Where are you going? When will you return?"

He stared at her for a long, disturbing, soul-crushing moment before he covered the distance between them. Still reclining on the chaise, she waited with bated breath, her heart hammering behind her rib cage.

He would surely cut her to pieces for asking that question, for assuming such…

Kneeling down to her level, he took her hand in his. Her hand was delicately slender in his huge one, and suddenly, she felt a sense of security she hadn't known in a long time. It was as if a fuzzy feeling unspooled in her gut.

"I have a very irate portfolio manager that I have to mollify after my latest bout of shopping frenzy," he whispered, and she laughed through the weariness.

"Tonight I can sleep, can't I? For as long as I want?"

He squeezed her hand, and she thought how rough his palm was. "Yes, you can, Jas. No one will come in. You're…safe here."

Her eyelids felt as if they would glue together forever. Jas squeezed his hand back and whispered, "Thank you," before giving in to the sleep claiming her.

Maybe she didn't have to hate Dmitri so thoroughly, the

thought came to her. She would still pay him back, yes, but they could at least be friends, couldn't they?

As much friends as she could be with a man who had bought her and who set her pulse racing like nothing in life ever had.

A man who was making it harder for her to hate him.

CHAPTER FIVE

DMITRI RETURNED WELL past eleven, his entire morning spent in a fruitless search. He still had no answers whatsoever as to what Noah had intended. He had been shut down at every avenue he had pursued and he knew why. Noah didn't want word getting out about Jasmine getting out of her debt. Even though the greedy old bastard had milked the occasion for all its worth.

Bad for his business.

And he knew he could expect no answers from the infuriatingly deceptive woman herself.

There were too many unknowns about what she had done these past few years. And then there was her assumption that he had never looked back for Andrew or her.

Even though he had.

Andrew had been viciously angry with Dmitri that last time they had met, just months before he had died, because Dmitri had refused to give him any more money. Because Dmitri had wrongly hoped that cutting Andrew off after so many years would curb his gambling habit.

He had never thought Andrew would poison Jasmine against him, however, that he would lie about all the times Dmitri had lent him money.

But then he shouldn't have been shocked. Didn't he know firsthand the consequences of addiction and self-loathing it built up? How it only looked for a scapegoat?

For years, Dmitri had faced his father's fists just because his father hadn't been man enough to accept that his alcoholism had been responsible for the miserable state of their lives. No, his cowardly father had blamed his mother instead.

After everything he and Andrew had been to each other, Dmitri had become that scapegoat for Andrew.

No wonder Jasmine despised him. And he had no intention of telling her the truth, either. He needed the distance her hatred for him put between them.

But the sense of honor Giannis and Stavros had instilled in him wouldn't let him wash his hands of her.

It meant he couldn't just pad her bank balance and remove her from his life. Not until he figured out this whole auction mystery about her. Not until he was completely sure that Jasmine could walk away from that life.

Unbuttoning his shirt, he entered the bedroom and stilled.

The blinds were open and the sunlight made every inch of the room glitter with a soft, golden glow.

And in the middle of it, on the chaise longue, lay Jasmine. Her hands were folded under her cheek, her long legs half dangling on the other side revealed delicate feet with red-tipped toes.

She was only a few inches shorter than him, which meant she had to be uncomfortable as hell on the chaise. While a perfectly good king-size bed lay in touching distance.

Stubborn woman!

If not for sheer exhaustion, she would have crawled out to the corridor rather than take his help, he knew.

Without intending to, he found himself moving closer to her.

Her dark hair was finally out of the knot and spread against the beige upholstery like nightfall, lustrous and wavy. Spiky eyelashes curved against her cheeks, her plump, wide mouth, for once not pursed in disapproval.

She looked like a wild, beautiful horse he had once seen on Stavros's farm, a horse that had refused to be mounted by anyone. An incongruous, irresistible combination of untouched innocence and untamed wildness.

One minute, she was consigning him to hell for his sins and more, the next, melting into him.

He sank to the floor and leaned his head against the bed, memories he had locked away rushing at him.

He didn't remember a moment of his childhood without her in it.

She had been such a tall, gangly little girl when he had left, her black eyes filled with fat tears when she had said goodbye.

For years, after he had moved in with Giannis, he remembered that face and her wet kiss on his cheek.

Even now, at first glance, she looked scrawny, the robe sticking on her angular shoulders, drowning her lithe form. But that was where the girl he remembered with such fondness ended.

Honey-gold and smooth, her skin shone with a brilliance no amount of makeup could achieve, transforming her face. There was a lean, tensile strength to her body, a fluid grace and energy that had slammed into him when he had tackled her.

Curves that had pressed against his forearm that he couldn't see now...

Theos, was he so shallow that he was this desperate for a peek at what she so desperately wanted to hide? Had he truly become that playboy who had the hots for every woman that came into his life?

Was there nothing he wouldn't take to sate that perpetual emptiness within him?

Because, for once, Stavros was wrong, his faith in Dmitri misplaced. There was something between Jasmine and him, and every inch of him wanted to explore what it was, and she...she was no match for him.

Theos, this was Andrew's little sister, the last woman he needed to tangle with, however much she made him feel things he had never felt before.

He pushed himself off the floor, called Reception and requested a different suite.

He had plans for tomorrow, for next week, for the next month. And he intended to keep those plans.

And that meant the bachelor party he was throwing Stavros at a strip club in Monaco. Something he had been looking forward to ever since Stavros had pronounced that he was marrying Leah again, properly this time.

By the end of the next three days, Jasmine was ready to throttle Dmitri with her very hands. And more than annoyed with herself for being a naive idiot.

She had woken up long past midday, feeling as if a speeding bus had run her down. Her body was a mass of bruises from being tackled by the giant brute, her neck ached from sleeping at an awkward angle for so long on the chaise longue, which she kicked out of a perverse anger when she was up, and of course, her foot hurt because of that.

The worst was the feeling of being caged in the sophisticated but deafeningly silent hotel suite. What had seemed so secure in the dark of the dawn now felt like a jail that cut her off from the rest of the world.

Looking out of the French windows, she had seen the bustle of Bond Street and yet, she felt worlds away.

She hadn't minded it so much the first day, having spent two hours soaking in the decadent marble tub. Not even when the hotel physician and a nurse had arrived, *on the orders of Mr. Karegas of course*, to ensure Ms. Douglas suffered no ill effects after the stress of her previous day.

Not when she had been served a five-course meal with as much aplomb as if she were the queen.

In fact, she had been impressed and softened and whatnot by the time she'd finished her chocolate-dipped strawberries and mint tea. Even convinced herself that she had been extremely stupid in not coming to Dmitri for help sooner.

By the evening of the second day, she was ready to hitch herself up on the prestigious artwork and climb the walls.

So dressed again in her freshly laundered old jeans and one of Dmitri's Savile Row dress shirts—she couldn't bear to even look at her old sweater—she had stepped out of the suite and found a hulking giant following her down the corridor and into the lift.

He had appeared by her side as she waited for the doorman, his hand on her wrist sending a current of fury through her.

"You're not to leave the premises of the hotel, miss," he had replied when she had glared at him. "Mr. Karegas ordered that you stay put until he's sure you're safe," he had said with a repressive shudder.

Flushing as if she had been caught out being particularly naughty, she had mumbled off something and dutifully headed back into the room. Only later had she realized that Dmitri had practically made her a prisoner.

Even then, she had warmed up, so devoid of basic security her life had been.

So she had waited, over the next day and another day. Patiently and with even a growing sense of gratitude and warmth, her gullible, ever-ready-to-succumb-to-temptation mind painting pictures of their blossoming friendship.

Until she had surfed the channels and seen the latest tabloid channel report.

Dmitri Karegas was living it up at the illustrious bachelor party he was throwing his best friend and business partner of years, Stavros Sporades.

Hadn't Leah said she was Stavros's wife?

The feature went on to talk about the world-famous strip club, the hundred different champagnes that had been served, a burlesque show that apparently was the raciest thing ever and the sexiest, the most raucous bachelors from the world attending, including a Hollywood movie star, a sheikh from the middle east and a Japanese media mogul…and Dmitri Karegas.

Stavros, the supposed groom, Jasmine realized, was conspicuously absent.

Somehow, she had a hard time imagining that austere, almost forbidding man giving in to the kind of excesses that would go on at the party that feature boasted about.

Because her job had given her ample exposure to it, especially when she had waitressed at a private party once, too terrified of taking on her usual duties.

Drinks, dancing, women…and Dmitri, with his reputation for a voracious sexual appetite in the middle of it all…

Her gut heaved so violently at the very thought that she pressed her hand to it…

What the hell was wrong with her? She was acting as if they were…

No, she wouldn't even think it.

Two photos of the party had been leaked through the usual social media sites.

One showed two buxom blondes—really there was no other way to describe the décolletage of the two women—corralling him on either side, holding their empty champagne flutes aloft while Dmitri popped the cork open with a thousand-kilowatt smile for the flashing camera bulbs.

The second one was a close-up of him, a grainy shot clicked with a cell phone camera. Those hauntingly beautiful eyes of his held a smirk...a challenge? A chasm of emptiness that she wished she understood...

Did no one else get glimpses of the man she did? It felt as if only she could see beneath the mask he wore to the real man.

Something swelled in her chest, so intense was her longing to understand him again like she had once.

Her cell phone's chirp, a text from her mother pleading with Jas for any cash she could spare, pulled her from the trance. A technologically delivered slap to pull her back to her reality, so to speak.

Of course, Dmitri wasn't worried about her. It was nothing but a ruse to scare her into staying put just so he could feel better about his unwanted duty toward her.

Hadn't she started this whole thing because she didn't want to be anyone's prisoner?

There was an ongoing...*negotiation* between Dmitri and her, that was all.

A string of softly spoken words, a kind glance and some pasta Alfredo and she was ready to turn into his next groupie.

He owed her nothing, having paid a thousand times over. He had clearly told her that she was but an inconvenience, ordered her to stay on the periphery of his life.

Where was this sense of betrayal coming from then? *Dear Lord*, how desperate was she for some kind of connection that she projected it onto the first man who had looked at her with nothing but a begrudging kindness? One who had been disgusted by her lifestyle?

The next two hours she spent in the suite waiting for the giant security guard to change shifts was the longest of her life. The minute the clock struck four, she grabbed her handbag, stepped into the lift and ran out of the building.

If she hurried, she could make it to her bank on time and withdraw cash for her mum.

Ten minutes into walking into the neighborhood she grew up in, unease gripped Jasmine.

Something sinuous settled in her belly at the thought of going back to her dinky flat. *No*, it wasn't the flat as much as it was the life she didn't want to lead anymore.

She needed to start a new chapter in her life. Needed to use this time to make a clean break of it, once and for all.

Tomorrow, she would start looking for a new job. As soon as she thought it, her heart sank. The only connections or contacts she had were the ones revolving around the nightclub, her brother's friends and Noah's men.

Except for Dmitri.

Dmitri, who it seemed could turn her inside out just by existing.

She spent the next few hours running errands—withdrawing cash, buying groceries and mulling over new career possibilities that would help her earn a hundred thousand pounds fast enough. And catching quite a bit of gossip at her old haunts.

Apparently, the fact that Dmitri had bought her was something of news in their little flea-infested, junkie-ridden neighborhood and she was the star of the feature. The almost envious lewdness that dripped from the comments that in the end she would go in the same career route as her mother, of course with a bit of an upgrade to it, what with Dmitri being a billionaire and all, had been extremely hard to swallow.

Had she thought she was better off here for even a minute? She had no education, no job training, and she knew nothing except keeping herself in good shape and keeping her head down. Hours of rigid exercise and practice had made her a good pole dancer, but what other job could use that?

Her skin clammy with sweat, she packed a quick bag, stuffing in underwear, another pair of jeans, a few blouses and the few cosmetics that she owned.

And the diamond pendant, her one precious belonging, that Andrew had given her for her eighteenth birthday.

This was it.

She was saying goodbye to this life. Her pride and her curious weakness when it came to Dmitri… She would have to find a way to deal with it.

It was past eight when she finally reached her mum's flat. The same frustration built up inside her as she borrowed the keys from old Mrs. Davies, but this responsibility, Jasmine realized, she couldn't walk away from. Not until one of them was dead.

She cleaned up the one-bedroom flat, emptied the grocery bags and then loaded up the cardboard boxes with empty bottles. She put the check she had made out at the bank in an envelope and left it on the counter.

The bulky box in hand, she had barely made it down the steps when the hairs on her neck stood up, like the antenna on her mother's old TV.

The long lines of a dark limo slowly materialized under the sadly flickering streetlight, the sleek vehicle a stark contrast against the dirty pavement.

And leaning against it, his long coat fluttering against the wind, his denim-clad legs crossed at his ankles, stood Dmitri. Moonlight illuminated his face in shadows and strips but still enough for her to see the arctic blaze in his eyes.

Soundlessly, he moved toward her and Jasmine let out a yelp, trying to escape him.

The cardboard box slipped from her fingers and thudded to the ground, the bottles causing a loud tinkling sound. Anything she had been about to say fell away from her in a horrified squeak as he lifted her off the ground, threw her over his shoulder, waited for his chauffeur to open the door.

And then threw her onto the long leather seat as if he was dumping out yesterday's garbage.

Undignified protests sputtering from her mouth, she had barely even straightened on the seat when the limo took off.

"What the hell do you..."

The dark scowl etched on his brow shut her up instantly, his silver-plated watch glinting in the dark as he barked out commands in Greek.

Jasmine pressed her fingers to her temple and forced herself to breathe in and out. She sat up straight and looked out the window, struggling to rein in her temper. Of course, the tinted glass offered up a reflection of the man's aquiline nose, sculpted cheeks and a mouth made for sin.

He didn't get off the phone all through their drive through the city. They had left her dirty neighborhood, drove for a long while and finally had crossed the motorway when the limo came to a stop. Even then, he didn't look at her. Only waited patiently when the door was opened.

Jasmine scrambled out with as much dignity as she could muster, given that he was dragging her with him as if she were a recalcitrant child.

"Oh, wow..." she said, as she finally noticed the sleek lines of the jet that was already idling. Glancing around only now, she saw the acres of empty land stretched out on all sides, a string of lights marking a couple of runways. They were at a private airstrip, miles away from the city.

She pulled at her arm. His fingers dug into her flesh.

"Ow, ow... Dmitri, you're hurting me."

He let her go so suddenly and with such force that she half stumbled. She couldn't believe it was the same man who had fed her pasta with such tenderness. "What is wrong with you?" she yelled.

Fury gripped his features. "You were not supposed to leave the hotel suite. There was a report of a young woman's body found near the..."

Turning around, he kicked at the ground, causing asphalt to fly around them.

She put her hand on his arm and he tensed. "I was never in any danger."

"*Theos*, Jas, do you want to go back to that life? Is that it? You're just as addicted to the danger and desperation of it as him? Like the whole infernal lot of people I've been cursed to know?

"If you are, tell me now. Because I won't have your death on my conscience, too."

Andrew. He was talking about Andrew, Jas realized slowly—about Andrew's lifelong gambling addiction.

How long had he known? Had he found out after he had talked to Noah?

But Jasmine couldn't bring his name up. Not when the very subject of Andrew seemed to push them both into a dangerous territory. Not when she didn't trust herself to say something nasty just because Dmitri was here and her brother wasn't.

Dmitri had had a benevolent godfather who had come for him just at the right time, true. But the whole world knew how hard he and Stavros had worked to turn their godfather's small factory into a global empire.

While Andrew had only continued to make worse and worse choices.

"I'm not Stavros. I won't save someone against their own wishes to self-annihilate, Jas. If I walk away now, I will never come back."

"No, I don't want to go back," she answered, all her fury fizzling out at the anguish in his words. "Not for a day. I was angry that you…" Her claim sounded so childish to her own ears. It wasn't his fault that she was feeling so fragile.

She met his gaze squarely. "I only went back to collect a few things, Dmitri. I was going to beg you to…" She paused, realizing she hadn't actually come up with a plan except to throw herself at his mercy.

Again.

"Beg me for what?"

"A job. Or something."

His fury shifted as he assessed her with disbelieving eyes. He ran a hand through his hair. "That's the first sensible thing you've said to me. And you wasted my entire evening."

She did seem to have a death wish, because the words poured out of her without the basic check her brain was supposed to engage. "An evening of more festivities in Monaco?"

Instantly his expression shuttered, changed. An infinitesimal moment in which she caught a glimpse of something, a hunger, beneath the surface. Just as she had seen in the photo in the newspaper.

When he looked at her again, the careless indifference was back in place. "My activities or my personal life is none of your business, so stay out of it."

When she dug in her feet, he turned around with a sigh. "And before you waste another few minutes, yes, your life, at least for now, is my business."

"How, except that I owe you money that I could never repay?"

"Five years ago, when Andrew died, I should have dragged you out of that hellhole. I didn't, and that decision has cost me a hundred thousand pounds and an ever-increasing amount of havoc on my life. Until I ensure you won't end up on the streets again, you'll stay with me."

Oh, how she wanted to smack the arrogance off his

face, but he was right. She had nowhere to go. So she followed him up the stairs and into the...most luxuriously chic aircraft she had ever seen.

Hanging on to her foolish pride because really, no one could expect her to get used to this kind of wealth when she had lived hand to mouth all her life, she tried very hard to act as if she traveled in first-class luxury with a textile tycoon every other day.

If the outside of the Learjet was all sleek lines and thrumming power, the inside was world-class spacious luxury she had only ever seen in glossy magazines. Power seats in cream leather so soft that she was scared of scratching it sat in two different clusters with legroom enough to accommodate a giraffe. *Or her.*

Two flat-screen monitors whirred out of the ceiling as she watched while the flight attendant rattled off a wine selection, half of which she had never even heard of. Sparkling water was all she had ever allowed herself, before, during or after work, resolved to never blunt her senses in any way.

"Just water for me, thanks," she finally said, just to stop the woman from figuring out she wasn't Dmitri's usual caliber guest.

The moment the thought crossed her mind, she felt ashamed of herself. That she wasn't sophisticated or educated had never bothered her before.

"Where are we going?" she asked when they settled down.

"We're not returning. Not unless my business dictates it. You'll travel with me until I...until you get back on your feet. But not in London, not when you'll only be tempted to go back to that life."

Her mum hadn't cared about Andrew or her for as long as she could remember. Only about her broken dreams and drowning them in alcohol...

Even Andrew's legacy for her had been crushing debt, debt that had turned her life in a direction she had never wanted it to take.

"There's something to be said for a clean break, Jas. Believe me."

Jasmine exhaled roughly, realizing he was right. "Can you please have someone check in on my mum once in a while?"

"Already taken care of."

Her nerves jangled with excitement and fear and so many more feelings she couldn't name. But at least there was no regret for the life she was leaving behind.

CHAPTER SIX

DMITRI HAD NEVER considered the private jet owned by Katrakis Textiles small by any standard before tonight. It was not his favorite, as anything—bike, car or flight—that boasted size over speed wasn't.

But the spacious front cabin with a king-size bed in the rear had served him well on his cross-Atlantic trips, especially when he was traveling on business with a team in tow.

The constantly fidgeting woman sitting across from him, however, made him reconsider this view.

She was making him reconsider too many decidedly sure things he had designed for his life, things that gave him shallow and transient pleasure at the least, things he had become used to...

Theos, he had looked forward to that bachelor party for months.

But the weekend in Monaco had turned out to be torturously boring for him, his mind pushing the picture of Jasmine sleeping so peacefully in his bedroom, to the fore.

There was something utterly satisfying about keeping her safe. And after his failure to save his mother, he didn't misunderstand where the feeling came from, either. But even then...

The sight of a woman had never transfixed him like that.

Like a treasure that called to seamen, luring them, her

stunning face had come to him in the strangest of moments, stealing away whatever satisfaction the moment would have presented.

So here he was, his usually uncaring mood roused to a temper, his libido unsatisfied, while the confounding woman's presence in his life spread as if it was a stubborn virus.

The picture she presented, everything covered up from top to bottom, shouldn't have snagged his attention at all.

Her jeans, while obviously worn out and of cheap quality, were snug and tight, encasing her long, long legs like a glove.

He had received an eyeful of her mouthwateringly pert bottom while she had knelt in the seat and tugged viciously at the poor, unsuspecting seat belt, not realizing that all she had to do was to click on the latch for it to pull.

And then there was the real culprit that sent a simmering awareness through his blood for the sheer intimacy of it.

His pristine white, custom-made Armani dress shirt that she wore.

He was bulkier and broader and she was thin, waiflike… The shirt should have looked like a bag on her scrawny build.

The shoulder seam fell to her upper arms, while she had rolled up the sleeves. Tucked into those tight jeans, it billowed over her torso. But with the outline of her black bra visible through the thin cotton, the wide collar flashing peeks at golden honeyed skin every time she moved, it was the most erotically feminine thing he had ever seen.

Never had a woman so thoroughly covered up fired his curiosity to such depths.

She made his shirt her own in such a sexy way that he wanted to rip it off her, press his mouth to that silk-like skin, so that he could discover, for himself and for her, what lay beneath.

Theos, he was turning rock hard and he hadn't even touched her…

No other woman in the world had ever baffled Dmitri like her; no other woman shook his compass in such a shattering way.

Despite everything, there was an inner strength to Jasmine that scorched him every time he looked into her eyes. Add to that, that instant charge whenever she looked at him out of those big black eyes.

"Is your mother well?" he said, choosing a topic that would surely defuse that charge.

A line of tension immediately bunched her shoulders tight before she slowly turned toward him. Her mouth closed on the bottle as she took a long sip. His blood rushed south as a picture of that saucy mouth wrapped around him came forth…

He pressed his fingers to his temple, searching for a shred of decency.

"As fine as she can be." She screwed the cap back slowly. "Even Andrew's death changed nothing for her."

The bitterness in her tone took him aback first. Then it cycled to guilt and frustration.

He should have gone back for her after Andrew's death, shouldn't have walked away just because of his past failures. He knew, firsthand, the price a child paid for a parent's destructive addiction. Even if her mother's alcoholism had resulted in neglect of her children and not something much worse. A cold chill climbed up his spine. "Does she still—"

"Drink like a fish and then spiral into pitiful sobs remembering Andrew's dad and then mine in that order? Yep… The worst are the stories about me turning into some Arab princess overnight when my father comes back for her after all these years. Thinks it's going to be *Princess Diaries*—Jasmine-style."

Her smile too wide, the glitter in her eyes too bright, she looked as if she would break with a gentle tap. Tenderness like he had never known engulfed Dmitri. He didn't know what to do with it, didn't know how to stop feeling it.

He had no words of comfort to offer. "Do you want me to look for him?"

Shock widened her eyes. "My father?"

He nodded. "It might not be that hard now that—"

"He spun stories, used her for a year and skipped town the moment she told him she was pregnant. She was nothing but a convenient mistress for a visiting diplomat. He had twenty-four years to change his mind. I don't need another parent who looks at me as if I was the reason their life took a miserable turn."

"Then, why did you go to see her again?" Frustration mounted inside him. "Why were you running around all evening loading up groceries, cleaning up?"

She frowned. "I haven't checked on her in a week."

"How much did you end up giving her this time?"

Her neck moved this way and that, that ugly knot at the back of her head making his fingers itch with the urge to unravel it. She was stalling, he knew.

That run-down flat was in a dilapidated part of the city; the empty bottles she carried out, the way she had almost cringed into herself in the darkness... Image after image flashed in front of his eyes... *Theos*, how did you protect someone from their own naïveté?

Suddenly, he had newfound respect for what Stavros went through with Leah.

Studying her neatly trimmed nails, she cleared her throat. "You're making too much of..."

"How much, Jas?"

It felt as if a vein would burst in his temple, as if his very life was shifting in front of his eyes.

He hadn't meant to shout. He hadn't meant to get so

angry. He hadn't meant to spend every waking minute thinking of the infuriating woman or wanting to wring her neck. Or kiss her senseless.

"Just a little…" She swallowed when he continued to glare at her. "Okay, fine, most of what I saved. Her rent was overdue by two months and she had—"

His filthy curse rang around the cabin, but did nothing to alleviate his frustration.

Jasmine looked at him with wide eyes, more alert than shocked at his outburst.

"So all of the seven thousand pounds you were boasting about? No wonder you weren't making any dent in—"

"Yes, okay. I have done this before."

He shot up from his seat, like a wild animal that had forced itself to be peaceful until now. That was what always made her curious.

That carefree, reckless, unemotional demeanor he put on—that wasn't the natural state for Dmitri.

His jeans outlined those powerful thighs and tight butt, his gray shirt molding to the hard planes of his lean stomach. It was impossible to be in the same room as him and not be aware of his every breath, every movement.

Before she could blink, he was bending over her seat, his breath whispering against her cheek.

Every inch of her uncoiled at the latent power of his body caging her against the seat. Heat from his lean frame stroked her, and she gripped the leather seat tight. "You do know that she will just drink all your hard-earned cash, don't you?"

She nodded, mesmerized by the molten depths of his eyes.

"Then, it hasn't sunk into that stubborn skull of yours that she's only manipulating you? That she will suck the blood out of you but not stop? That you're nothing but a crutch that she'll use for the rest of your life?"

"She's still my bloody mother." She was shouting now, her eyes filling with furious tears. "Would you rather I walk away like you did, wash my hands off, turn away from that dirty world? Pretend as though I never came from there in the first place, as if I never had a weakness or a flaw to begin with? Spend the rest of my life pursuing mindless pleasure in every corner of the world as if it was my due?"

A flicker of something molten flashed in his eyes, a flinch to his mouth.

She had surely angered him now. But instead of fear, she felt only exhilaration. As if the blood pounded harder in her veins.

He dipped his head even lower, bringing his mouth so close to hers. *God*, all she had to do was tilt her chin up and her lips would graze his. She would finally know how he tasted; she would know what she had already imagined a thousand times over.

Just one taste, that was all she wanted of this man who set her senses aflame without even trying.

"So whatever little you had to pay me back is gone now, *ne*?" he finally said in a silkily dangerous voice.

It made her feel oddly hollow, weightless.

"What happened to your pride, Jas? What happened to paying me back even if it killed you? What happened to not depending on me for anything ever again?" His thumb traced her lower lip, as if he was testing the shape and softness of it.

It was not affectionate or tender…and yet, the ache between her legs was long, low and instantaneous.

Instead of slamming his hand away, she froze.

"You don't have a job. You donated your meager savings because you're weak enough to still want to matter to her." He traced the seam of her collar with a long finger, and her skin tingled as if he had drawn a line of fire down her throat. "Even the shirt you're wearing is mine." Her heart threatened to rip out of her chest as he scrunched the fabric with one hand and pulled her forward.

He whispered the words against the corner of her mouth. "How exactly do you think you're going to pay me back now that you're penniless?"

Incendiary heat sparked from that small patch of skin, and she shivered violently. His fingers pressing into her jaw, his body locking her against the seat, there was nowhere for her to go, even if she would have wanted to.

"Or is it that," he continued, a certain relish to the way he enunciated every word, "your pride and outrage at being in my debt was just an elaborate farce? Did you envision living a cozy and comfortable life off my goodwill and wealth? A rich benefactor was what you were looking for all along? Does Noah get a cut?"

She felt her chest tighten at the very picture he painted in such a honeyed tone, as if he very thoroughly relished twisting the knife as deep as he could.

A soundless scream ricocheted inside her, leaving marks, while she still grappled with the poison in his words, with that savagely satisfied glint in his gaze.

He's doing this on purpose, some naive, weak part of her moaned.

But she squashed that stupid, wanting, weak Jas.

It didn't matter how much he believed his own outrageous claim; it didn't matter if he truly thought her a scheming witch out to snare a better lifestyle.

What mattered was that he had chosen to say those words out loud, that with every word he spoke, with every look he cast at her, Dmitri pushed her away, hated her very presence in his life.

Dmitri, she realized with a painful breath, was so dangerous to her. All she wanted at that moment was to pay his debt, walk out of his life and never see him again. Never subject herself to this hollow weakness, to this constant shame and inadequacy clinging to her every pore.

And there was only one way she could do both: take something she seemed to want with a longing like she never had, and pay off his debt.

The only way, as crazily desperate as it was…

Clasping his cheek, she covered the last bit of distance between them. Pressed her mouth against his, her teeth grinding against his lips. A tremendous stillness came over him while an inferno of heat and shame and fury raged inside her.

She could feel her heart hammer against her chest, like a bullet would ricochet in a closed room, punching holes through it…

And then it slowed down as his gaze clung to hers, a palette of emotions burning through it.

His mouth…oh, that sinful mouth was so hot and soft, seemed to fit so perfectly against her…and everything inside her sobbed and reveled at how intoxicatingly good he tasted. Everything inside her wanted to sink and burrow into him… All this in the space of one jagged breath.

Time itself seemed to come to a screeching halt, and Jas slanted her mouth afresh against his again, arching into his body, and tasted him, again and again…this way and that, moving and lapping while his bristly chin scratched her, while his breath infused hers…

The scent and taste and heat of him exploded inside her and she wanted more of this madness; she wanted him to kiss her back if it was the last thing she knew, so she dug her teeth into that sculpted lower lip…

And he turned into a burst of violent energy around her. His fingers crawled into her hair, molded her scalp roughly and slammed her against him. Her breath shoved out of her lungs.

Sweet victory was hers, she thought, drowning in the storm in his gray eyes...

He growled against her mouth, hot and hungry. And her aching sex pulsed in tune with that feral sound. The sweep of his tongue, the biting grasp of his mouth... It was like a furnace had been stoked into life inside her.

His mouth clung to hers with an erotic heat. Pleasure suffused her every nerve until she thought she would burst from the inside out. That mouth—*oh, God, that mouth*—it devoured her softness, pressing and plunging, licking and nipping, biting and bruising, one hand splayed against her scalp, one hand holding her shoulder in a bruising grip so that she didn't lean into him.

A moan, drugged and delirious and, oh, so wicked, rang around the cabin, and she realized that it was she who made that sound. That she was panting and moaning, that a rush of wet heat filled her core, that an ache zoomed from her mouth to every inch of her, that Dmitri's kiss was more real, more him than anything else he did or said.

It was as if she had found the Dmitri that she had been waiting for all these years, here of all places.

In his kiss.

Her soft, tentative mouth was like pouring kerosene onto a thin flicker of fire, working him into such a state of arousal that Dmitri felt it burn his throat.

Then her tongue licked his lower lip and his erection became thick against his jeans, as if it could imagine those licks against itself...

It was unlike anything he had ever known in the past decade or with another woman. But it was the vulnerability that she strove so hard to hide in her eyes that captured him.

Her eyes held that perpetual longing for something, that same hungry look that he saw when he looked at himself in the mirror. Something inside her had always calmed him, and now it was as though the effect had grown up along with them, morphed into pure sexual hunger.

It stirred into fire that unquenchable hunger inside him, filled the void that resonated inside him whatever he did, however far he went to fill it...

She would be different, he knew. She would be an experience he would never forget in his life. She would be the drop that would finally quench his thirst.

Because Jasmine knew him, the real him. Not this charming, pleasure-seeking playboy that he had become to hide the reality.

And she would give him everything she had. He could see it in her eyes, in the way her eyes turned molten, in the way her mouth trembled when he came near.

What will happen after that, Dmitri? a voice very much like Stavros needled. *Christos*, that bastard had really become his conscience over the years, hadn't he?

And the voice that was full of honor and integrity poured ice-cold water over his lust. Black, guileless eyes wide, she stared at him with a sort of wonder. That very same look that had pulled him back from so many moments of rage.

Except now it was tinged with sexual need.

Hating himself, because her taste was already implanted in his very cells, he wrenched himself away from her. *Christos*, it wasn't working. Nothing he did to keep her at a distance was working.

"What the hell do you think you're doing?" Every word was gritted out through a tight jaw.

Jas tried not to flinch and failed, hurt and shame diluting the haze of desire in her blood. With shaking fingers, she touched her tingling mouth, wondering if she would ever forget the taste of him.

"I'm offering myself to you. I'm saying—" a balloon could be crushing her lungs "—take what you paid for."

She saw his flinch in the tightening of that concrete jawline, in the slow, almost imperceptible blink of his eyes, as if he was chasing away the shock before it could unsettle him completely. As if nothing he didn't allow himself to feel was to be borne.

He pushed away from her then, and it was that exaggerated, you-are-plague kind of movement that pricked her. "And what would that be, *agapita*? See, to this minute, I'm not sure what made Noah think you were worth that atrocious amount of money. What drove another man to bid for you against me?"

Crackling energy arced into life around them, but she was damned if she backed down now. "Have sex with—"

A flare of warning in his eyes arrested the word on her mouth. Coiled energy seeped from his very pores, as if his usual facade was surface-thin now. "Be careful what you say to me, Jas."

But she couldn't let him intimidate her now or he would do it forever, she realized. It seemed they were engaged in some kind of power play. God knew how, for she had nothing to take him on with, but no way was she going to back down. "Take my virginity. Call my debt done. God, let us walk away from this impossible situation."

"So you're selling yourself to pay off your—"

She slapped her hand over his mouth, a surge of fury washing through her. "Don't say it, or this time I'll drive the knife deeper willingly."

His mouth was a furnace against her palm. Slowly, as if it took him a tremendous amount of willpower, he pushed it back. "Then, what is it you're proposing, *thee mou*?"

She looked away, struggling to marshal her thoughts. His taste still lingered on her lips; her scalp tingled with how hard he had held her.

Had it been a knee-jerk response, then, that kiss? Did men inevitably kiss back with such heat when a woman threw herself at them? Was Dmitri no different from all the other men whose lust was so easily inspired by naked flesh grinding a pole?

The thought made her more than a little sick. But the kiss had felt so personal, as though she was getting a part of Dmitri...

It was tragic how little she knew. Although she had a feeling it wouldn't have come in handy with someone like Dmitri. It had been a week now since he had rescued her and yet she had no measure of him. At all.

"I'll sleep with you once. Just once to get even." Somehow, she held his gaze without betraying herself. "I won't be your mistress, Dmitri."

"You're automatically assuming that you fit the role of my mistress, *thee mou*. You don't. So don't lose sleep over it."

She barely resisted the urge to catch a glimpse of herself in the huge flat-screen monitor as his words ballooned inside her. She knew she was unfit for a lot of things, but this... *"I'm not...fit to be one?"*

"You're not my type."

"I thought anything with a set of boobs was your type."

His gaze dipped to her chest and stayed there, the most unholy light in it. As if he was asking her to give him a peek.

Heat claimed her face, and she folded her arms repressively. She knew what would wipe that look off his face, and for a self-indulgent second, she was so tempted to do it, but...her mouth went dry just at the thought of it.

"How would you know what I prefer, Jasmine?" Nice and pleasant and warm, as if they were discussing the weather.

"The tabloids are full of your manly exploits, as they like to call them. Orgies and parties aboard your yacht, motorbike races, boxing matches with other men who have to thump and pummel each other to prove their stick is bigger than everyone else's—"

His sudden laughter filled the cabin and she stared hard. The man was so unfairly gorgeous...

"Your very lifestyle is providing an economy for some of these magazines."

"And you were spending your hard-earned cash on them?"

She was trapped and they both knew it. "I want to hear about these standards of yours. I want to hear what screening process the most self-indulgent, pleasure-seeking playboy in the world has for the women he—"

"I like my women wanton, willing and experienced. I like them stylish and sophisticated and full of confidence in and out of bed." So basically, everything she was not, she realized. "I like them to want me in bed as if I was air."

Oxygen seemed to be fading fast as he enunciated each word, his gaze full of molten hunger. Her skin tingled; her body ached.

"I like to not wonder if I would find a knife in my back while I'm kissing her or to be wished to hell while I'm moving inside her."

"I would never knife you from the back," she mumbled, her mouth drying at the erotic picture he painted.

His mouth curved into one of those rarely genuine smiles. "That is true. Should I continue?"

"No."

"You're prickly, infuriatingly naive," he said it as if it was the most boring list in the world. "You have a lust/hate thing going on with me and...your virginity means you'll be high maintenance in bed."

"I do not have a lust/hate thing going on for you... What the hell do you mean, high maintenance?"

Damn it, she needed to find a way to stop his words from finding purchase inside her. Or a way to stop her body from wanting him so much...

Because no amount of twisting the truth was going to help her.

She wanted Dmitri with a hunger that knew no reason or rhyme. She wanted him to look at her as if she was the only woman on earth; she wanted him to worship her, look at her as if he couldn't breathe if he didn't have her.

For years, she had lived, cloaking herself in shame, unable to look at any man and not hate herself. It was the only way, clutching that self-disgust, that she had been able to go on.

The only way she had been able to slip into the skin of *Jazmin*, the pole dancer, and still face herself in the mirror come morning.

Now it was as though that shame was beginning to slide off her skin. Now it was as if she could breathe and face herself in the mirror again. For the first time, she could be a woman.

It was as if her sexuality, denied and deprived for so long, was on wings.

"Yes. I'll have to teach you what to do, be gentle so that you're not hurt, and then after the whole thing," he drawled, as if it was the hardest thing to sleep with her, "I'll have to hold you and mop your tears and lie that it was the most beautiful thing ever. Deflowering virgins is highly overrated, Jasmine.

"I like my sex fast, rough and without any accompanying drama, whereas you're an emotional cannon waiting to go off. And as you seem to know very well, I'm incapable of anything but the most insubstantial of emotions."

"I'm not an emotional cannon."

He undid his cuffs and rolled back the sleeves. Plump veins ran over the muscular arm, the sight of coarse hair on that olive skin giving her a warm flush. "In the past week, you have knifed me, sobbed all over me, tried to kiss me and wanted to cuddle as though I was your favorite—"

"Only an utterly ruthless bastard would count those against me in such a way."

"If you think I'm anything else, then you're more foolish than I thought, Jas. Find another way to pay me back."

"So that until then you will tug me along with you as if I was a pet you decided to keep while passing judgment on the choices I have had to make to survive."

"Yes, that's the one upside to this whole thing. I can tell you, repeatedly, what a naive, stubbornly annoying…" He looked away as if his fury couldn't be contained by words.

"You almost sound as if you care."

"And you sound far too desperate to hear that I care. *I don't care*, Jas. My only interest is in keeping you alive. I don't like even a pinprick of guilt, marring my lifestyle. So me looking after you is for purely selfish reasons."

Could he not leave her even a fragment of her pride? But for once, Jasmine had a feeling it wasn't about her, her shame, her nonexistent self-esteem.

Why was he always making sure she didn't form an attachment to him? Why did he insist on reiterating what he didn't feel for her?

What if it wasn't about her?

She looked around the plane, thought of the bike, the hotel he had taken her to. His yacht, his expensive toys, his women… If Dmitri was the playboy he played so well, he wouldn't have come for her like that.

If he hadn't cared, he wouldn't have been so angry

with her, then or tonight when she had suggested a way to pay off her debt.

"Is it so hard to admit that you feel something for me, Dmitri? Even if it was just an echo of our horrible past life together? Everything has to be this sanitized, sterilized version of you?"

His head recoiled back, tension swathing his entire frame. As though she was a danger to him. When he looked at her, his head cocked and eyes narrowed, Jas didn't buy it.

It was as if a storm was brewing in his eyes as he stood up. "That Dmitri was violent and deranged, Jas."

She had shocked him. Into what, she had no idea, but she had. Satisfaction swelled inside her. "At least that Dmitri was real."

"You're like that mutt Andrew saved once, remember? Even after it got better, he wouldn't go away. Kept coming back to him, desperate for another nuzzle."

Instead of the smooth, uncaring tone that he delivered all his insults in, he sounded ragged, on the edge, furious.

And just like that, his insults didn't hurt anymore.

Instead, she felt victorious, as if she had drawn him out finally.

Feeling more out of control of her own fate than her worst working nights had been, she sighed. "You said Stavros was Leah's husband. Are they really getting married again?"

"Stavros married Leah under the worst of circumstances." His voice took on a softer tone when he spoke of Leah. "To make up for it, he is giving her a wedding now."

"He looked so stern and forbidding…but he's doing it for her? That is so romantic. No wonder Leah looks as if she's glowing from the…"

His pointed look told Jasmine clearly what he thought

of her gushing. A burn began to climb up from her chest to her throat.

"Is that what you want, Jas?" he said without scorn or mockery.

"What I want... I've never even had the indulgence to think of what I want from life. It doesn't mean I can't appreciate someone else's happiness. Despite what I've had to do to survive, there's some innocence left inside me, Dmitri."

"Some innocence, Jas?" A light came on in his eyes, rendering Jas still. As if she had gained a little traction with him. Just a little but enough. "Have I been duped in the quality of my purchase? Is there a return tag, then?"

It was an outrageous situation they seemed to be caught in. And it was of their own making, too, Jas realized with a hollowness in her gut. But neither of them, it seemed, would walk away.

And if she didn't laugh, she was afraid she would cry. Or do something equally disastrous, like wanting to prove that she was woman enough for the arrogant rogue in front of her.

Prickly and high maintenance? Oh, how she wanted to do something that broke that smugly satisfied smile. How she wished she could shatter that facade of careless debauchery...

How she wanted him to kiss her, not because she thrust herself at him, not because he thought he should teach her a lesson, but because he wanted to, more than anything in the world.

Nothing more self-destructive in wanting to prove that she had a place in a man's life when he couldn't give a flying fig about it... She had seen her mother do it and had the worn-out child *and* adult T-shirts to wear for it.

"One of these days, you're going to wish you had sent

me on my way, Dmitri," she said, because empty challenges didn't cost anything.

She was far too invested in this strange relationship they had, she realized, fresh panic blooming in her gut.

CHAPTER SEVEN

JASMINE HAD NEVER imagined that she could feel lonely surrounded by at least a hundred guests at the estate where Stavros and Leah were getting married. It seemed as if the entirety of Athens' high fashion society was attending the party that night and would stay for the wedding.

Dmitri had dumped her once again at the estate in the middle of the night and disappeared after he had blurted out, "We'll talk about your future after the wedding."

He had quite literally handed her over to a maid and stormed back into the night.

Clamping her teeth so tight that it hurt, she had forced her mind away from where, and whose bed, he would be going to in the middle of the night.

Having fallen asleep at some strange hour of predawn, she had woken up this morning to the sounds of guests having a lazy, laughing breakfast in the courtyard outside her balcony. Disoriented by the amount of jet-setting she seemed to be doing, she had pulled on a sweater and ventured out to see Stavros and Leah and an assortment of strangers staring up at her.

It was obviously too early and too domestic a setting for Dmitri to be anywhere near.

She had never felt so out of place as that morning.

Yet what was he supposed to do with her, she had asked herself on her walk that afternoon. She was neither a friend for him to voluntarily want to spend time with her, nor was she a girlfriend, which would have been altogether another matter. Nor was she a family member.

She only wished he hadn't brought her to such an intimate occasion. The last thing she wanted to do was to intrude on Leah and Stavros.

She couldn't bear to think about what the couple thought of her. Because, despite everything, she liked them, and in a different life, she would have wanted them to like her.

Granted, she had spent barely any time with them and under such strange circumstances that night, but there had been such a familial bond between Dmitri and the two of them. A bond she had only seen once before, between her brother, Andrew, and Dmitri.

Had she somehow expected the same bond to exist between her and Dmitri, despite his new life and her supposed hatred for him? Was that why it felt as though she was being knocked down by every small thing he did or didn't do?

So she mostly kept herself to her room and walked around the lush acreage whenever she couldn't bear to stare at the elegant furnishings anymore. She had just finished walking through the vineyard and returned to her room when someone knocked on her door.

Leah Sporades stood outside the room. "May I come in?"

"Of course." Jasmine stood back, remembering her manners.

"I'm sorry I haven't been able to spend time with you after you arrived last night. I had so many last-minute details to look over and then of course, Stavros is being his usual arrogant, domineering—"

"Please, Leah, stop." Jasmine was equal parts embarrassed and amazed by Leah's openness. "Don't say another word. I should be the one apologizing for intruding on such a private and important occasion. You're not responsible for unexpected guests who crash in the middle of the night."

"What?" Now the woman looked genuinely baffled. "Jasmine, I insisted that Dmitri bring you. What did he say to you to make you feel as if you were not welcome…" Leah sighed. "He just dropped you here and left, didn't he? In the middle of the night?"

Jasmine decided she would rather die before she betrayed how much that had hurt. *Yet again.* "Yes, but then that's to be expected. It's not as if he's my keeper despite the fact that he… He insists on dragging me along but hates me for it… I don't understand why he won't just leave me to my fate."

The most painfully thick silence followed her outburst.

Jasmine turned away toward the window, mortification burning her face up as if it was a furnace. She had said way too much again.

Sighing, she pressed her forehead against the cool window. "Forget I said that, please. I…I'm usually not so whiny and self-pitying. The past few days, my life's taken the strangest turn after years of…" *And Dmitri was at the center of all the confusion…* "I feel a bit lost and directionless."

Leah joined her at the window and squeezed her hand.

Fighting a gush of warmth at the back of her eyes, Jasmine held on.

Her mom's lifestyle, Andrew's problems and then her own chosen path meant she had never had the chance to have a normal life. Now she realized how many small, simple things, like friendship, she had given up willingly along the way.

She hated him for it, but maybe there was credit to Dmitri's ruthless walking away from the whole lot of them. Cutting away those ties that only added burdens to her very soul. Starting afresh without the past hanging around her neck like a boulder.

He was flourishing, wasn't he? she thought with uncharacteristic envy.

"When Stavros told me what kind of a...situation Dmitri found you in, and how you got yourself out of it, I was amazed." Jasmine raised her gaze and met Leah's, the calm acceptance in her tone going a long way to soothe her. "What stuns me even more is how different and strangely intense Dmitri was around you in just those few minutes. Whatever is going on between you two—"

"Nothing is going on between us, Leah. I'm like that festering sore he wants to close, a dirty stain from his old life he wants to incinerate. In fact, I'm as stunned as you are with each passing hour why he won't just wash his hands of me. He's made it clear enough that this whole thing with me...has disrupted his life."

"But nothing ever disrupts Dmitri. Nothing even touches Dmitri. He has his work and toys. The only lasting relationship he has in his life is with Stavros, and he has that *insane*...lifestyle.

"Whereas with you, it's as if... He doesn't know what to do with himself with you around is what I'm thinking," Leah added, with a twinkle in her eyes that made Jasmine squirm uncomfortably.

Of course, she couldn't tell Leah it was all one-sided.

"You're so much in love," Jasmine said without rancor. "You're seeing rainbows and butterflies and possibility of romance where there is only guilt, Leah. Please don't matchmake."

"Am I that transparent?" Leah said. "All I wanted to say, Jas—I can call you Jas, right?" When Jasmine nodded, she went on, "Is that I know how it feels to not have a friend. And to deal with a man who, at least, *seems* to not like..."

"*Hate* is the word you're looking for," Jasmine pointed out sourly.

"*Hates* the very air you breathe," she said pointedly, and something in her gaze told Jasmine how far Stavros and Leah had to have come. "And turns you inside out. And makes you wish you were anyone but yourself."

Jasmine smiled, something in the other woman's openness catching up to her. "I don't believe Stavros could ever hate you. Even I can see that he worships you."

A blush dusted her cheeks and Leah laughed self-consciously. "But we almost lost each other. The thing is, you have a friend in me. And it has nothing to do with Dmitri."

Jasmine had never known such open acceptance, such genuine warmth. "Thank you."

Walking into the center of the room, Leah looked at her wardrobe. "Now let's talk about something fun. What are you wearing to the party tonight?"

Could one die of an excess of embarrassment? Jasmine wondered for the *n*th time in the past week.

"I...I don't have anything to wear. And I've had a lifetime's quota of being embarrassed and humiliated and whatnot by Dmitri."

Such an effervescent smile dawned on Leah's mouth that Jasmine forgot what she was going to say. "I'm a designer with an entire workroom full of dresses, and I would love to dress you in something that will knock the—"

Jasmine shook her head. "No, not for him," she amended.

What was the harm in borrowing a dress for one night? In opening herself to a friendship? In letting, for once, something good enter her life?

Whether willingly or not, Dmitri had given her her life back. And she was going to live it, for herself, starting tonight. Not her mother, not the pain of the past, not a debt, which somehow she would find a way out of, and definitely not about a man who kept her around because it relieved the little guilt he had about the past.

She faced Leah and smiled.

"I want to look good for myself. I want to have an evening where I forget the past week and don't worry about the future. I would love to borrow your expertise and your dress so that I can enjoy the party and be a part of my new friend's happiness. That sounds good, right?"

Leah beamed, hooked her arm through Jasmine's and said, "That sounds perfect."

Take what you paid for.

Jasmine's outrageous dare kept ringing around in Dmitri's head as he stepped out of his chopper and waved the pilot away.

And her kiss... *Theos*, it had lasted a few seconds too long, because he could still feel her taste on his lips, could still feel the liquid longing flowing through him.

As if she had left something of herself in his very blood.

He turned and stilled, taking in the tableau of the evening spread out from his vantage point atop the roof.

Giannis's estate, the very place that had shielded him and healed him, at least enough to move forward in life, was lit up like a bride. He was glad Leah had decided to have the wedding here. It would have made Giannis ecstatic to see Stavros and Leah begin their new life here.

A huge white marquee had been erected in the vast grounds behind the mansion. Soft, strategically placed ground lights lit up a path from the house to the marquee and all around the gazebo and the pool.

A profusion of stylishly dressed guests flitted in and out of the marquee, and he searched the festivities, only then realizing that he was looking for *her*. That all day, he hadn't been able to get her out of his mind.

Cursing himself, he walked off to shower and dress.

He had dropped off Jasmine past midnight and gone back to the Katrakis offices in Athens, the very force of his need to keep her by his side pushing him to do the opposite.

It had taken every ounce of his willpower, which was not much to begin with when it came to her, to keep rejecting her in the face of her increasingly reckless questions. In the face of her soft mouth flush against his, her breath coating his skin.

Take my virginity. Have sex with me, just once. Call the debt paid.

Something about the casually abhorrent way she had made that offer wouldn't leave him alone even now.

As if she was offering herself up like some sacrifice to circumstances beyond her help and he...he was *unscrupulous and monstrous* enough to want to take it.

It hurt him, he realized, stunned at the new development. It stung that she would think him low enough to take her under those conditions.

Did she think him so completely without morals? Hadn't he done all he could to make her think that?

But the farce he had begun sat like a knife under his ribs now, constantly pinching him. That she thought he was without morals or loyalty or even basic decency grated on him.

Theos mou, the more he tried to insult her and humiliate her and chain her with his words, the more she seemed to sink under his skin, the more she seemed to carve into him.

And the thing that boomed loud inside his head, refusing to be ignored, that had rattled him through the office hours today until he had walked out of a shareholder meeting that he had insisted on, was how tempted he had been to take her up on the disgusting offer.

Tempted to continue kissing her, to swallow her gasps and moans, to tear away the loose shirt and bare her to his gaze, to strip her until all that she worked so hard to hide was revealed to him...

Something desperate and needy inside him was mesmerized by her.

By her daring smile, by her disarming innocence, by her disquieting loyalty to her brother and mother, by her disturbingly sensual mouth that seemed to say the most outrageous things to him...

Having showered and dressed, he made his way back to the grounds, eagerly eating up the space. He spied Leah and Stavros at a distance chatting with a cousin of Giannis's who was an absolute bore, and grinned at the scowl that was beginning to make an appearance on his friend's brow when the younger man kept touching Leah.

Stavros, when it came to Leah, was like a dog with his favorite bone... No one would touch her if it was up to him, no one would even look at her...although for the first time since Dmitri had met Stavros, he began to understand Stavros's possessiveness.

Theos, he wished he didn't but he did.

He took a champagne flute from a passing waiter and downed it in one go, feeling decidedly on edge. Deciding he needed something stronger, he was about to walk toward the bar set up near the house when he heard husky laughter and turned toward the gazebo.

The vividly red curve of a woman's lush mouth met his gaze. Arrested, he stared, realizing slowly that it was none other than Jas.

Jas, as he had never seen or imagined her—exotic, stunning, brimming with a sensuality that had every drop of blood in him pounding south. Possessive desire knocked at him.

You're not my type.

You're prickly, you'll be high maintenance in bed.

Each and every one of his words came back to him as if fate had very neatly and viciously aligned them for him to swallow back.

She stood in the gazebo, a circle of light bathing her from head to toe. He noticed her shoulders first. A strange thing to be noticing about a woman, he instantly thought, the excellent champagne warming his throat.

Bare and delicately rounded, while her long arms had a muscle tone to them. His fingers itched to trace the graceful line of her neck to her collarbone.

Her hair, her glorious hair, finally free of that knot, framed her face in thick, wavy curls, softening that feral look.

A shimmering gold dress, with a neckline that crisscrossed over her breasts, pushed her breasts up and then, right below, flared out into billowing folds. It ended several inches above her knees, baring long, toned legs that literally went on forever.

For days, she had been covered up in the baggiest of clothes.

He had been right, she was far too much on the thin side, all jutting bones and sharp angles. But the shimmering fabric made everything of what there was of her.

She looked like an exotic bird; nothing so pedestrian as the word *beautiful* would suit her. A barely there chain hung over her throat with a glittering diamond pendant nestling in that cleavage.

Desire and possessiveness rolled through him in waves.

It felt like his stamp of possession that she wore a thing he had bought. Even though the simple fact that she was wearing the necklace proved that she clearly didn't know it. She would probably throw it in his face, he thought, grinning.

It had been mere months before Andrew had died,

for her eighteenth birthday. Dmitri had overseen his first million-dollar project and Giannis had made him a stockholder in the company. Two years after Stavros had made it. And had asked him how he wanted to celebrate. Looked at him with such a twinkling light in his eyes when Dmitri had said that he needed to buy a diamond pendant first.

What had he been thinking then? Had he always been waiting for her like this?

No, he told himself, discarding his champagne flute with a flick of his wrist. No, it had been about proving himself. He had wanted to go back to the one innocent in his old life and show her that he had made it. That he was nothing like the man who had raised him.

So he'd had it delivered, uncaring as to how Andrew would explain it. Something inside him roared in delight and he just couldn't silence it anymore.

Nothing ever touched him beyond an ephemeral satisfaction. Nothing ever held his attention for more than a few days.

Except now, with this woman. If her brother had kept him alive, it was as if she breathed new life into his very veins… As if she held the key to making him whole again.

When the man next to her bent too close to her, she tucked away a curl behind her ear in a nervous gesture.

And that hint of vulnerability tugged at Dmitri.

His hair slicked back, his narrow nose seeming all too familiar, the man stood far too close to her. When he turned, the light illuminated his profile, and Dmitri recognized him.

It was the French photographer, Gaspard Devue.

Devue's fingers moved over Jasmine's bare arm, trailed over her shoulder while she froze, her neck holding at an awkward angle, those large eyes of hers too big and trusting.

The bruises, the fear in Anya's eyes when she had come to his hotel in Paris... Gaspard Devue was one of those who preyed on the innocent, defenseless, who needed to use his fists to make himself feel bigger and stronger...

Just as his father had been...

Something detonated inside Dmitri at the thought of Jasmine even breathing the same air. All the sophistication he had acquired slid off him, and he was that fourteen-year-old boy who had finally had enough. Who had finally found enough strength in his lanky arms to defend himself, who had been terrified that one day he wouldn't get up after another blow.

That had been the last day his father had ever been able to touch him. But still, he had been too late to save his mother. Always too late.

Adrenaline punched through his blood, his muscles curling for a fight. It was all he could do to stop himself from marching over there and throwing her over his shoulder, from dragging her back to her room and locking her in...

He couldn't create a scene at Leah's party even if the bastard deserved it...

All he needed was to get Jas away from the man. And then he would lock her up for the next twenty years...

Christos, where was his head?

He didn't understand what was happening to him. He did, however, know what it was he wanted, craved. Sex and passion, he understood. That, for some reason, she trusted him and wanted him.

From the moment Giannis had pulled him away from that life, he had thought of her. He had been with countless women and hadn't felt an iota of what he felt when he just looked at Jas.

He wanted all of her.

* * *

She had known that he was watching her. Not from where or for how long. But the awareness had seeped into her as slowly as the breeze that caressed her bare shoulders, as sinuously as Leah's soft silk dress brushed against her skin, making her feel as if she, too, could be elegant and sophisticated instead of dirty and vulgar.

It was as though there was a chip under her skin that sent out a signal anytime Dmitri was close.

She had been so attuned to those sensations that she had missed half of what the suave Frenchman had said to her.

From the moment she had come down to the party, he had been so polite and attentive that Jasmine had felt flattered despite knowing that he was nothing but a seasoned flirt. Still, he had been telling her about all the photo shoots he had done with models she had only seen in magazines until she realized Dmitri was back and lost focus.

Belatedly, she caught him staring at her mouth and her face with a detached yet somehow intrusive intensity. Caught between embarrassment and hyperawareness, she froze when Gaspard trailed his fingers first over her jaw and then her neck. His strange gaze creeped her out more than the fact that he was touching her.

"So, *mademoiselle*, does my offer interest you?" he croaked out in a husky voice that felt just a little too practiced.

Schooling her face into a vacuous smile, she searched her mind for a way to ask the man what exactly his offer was. Because they had been talking about his studio, the project he took on, and if it was some kind of job or remotely like that, she didn't want to give offense.

And then she heard footsteps behind her—a soft tread like a predator that concealed its very ferociousness from an unsuspecting prey. Refusing to give in to the shiver that began at the base of her spine, she slowly turned, her hand still encased in Gaspard's.

The light from outside the gazebo enveloped him in a halo as he stood at the lower steps. Jasmine couldn't seem to breathe; her lips tingled, remembering, yearning.

A black tuxedo lovingly draped his broad shoulders, the snowy white collar contrasting against his olive skin. His freshly shaved jaw glinted and Jasmine once again felt the shocking awareness of every inch of space that Dmitri occupied.

He fairly breathed sex and masculinity and power, irrevocably out of her reach.

Until their eyes met. And then it was as though the world melted away around them. Every inch of skin that the silk touched felt hot; every muscle curled tight.

She reached out behind her, the wood grain smooth to her touch, hoping it would cool down this…heat inside of her.

He took the steps and a little chill pulsed down her back as his face was finally bathed in light.

Tight lines bracketed his mouth, that cool facade completely gone. His looks. His mood. His cloak of debonair charm. Everything had fallen away. Suddenly, he seemed like the Dmitri she had known once, and it tripped all her alarms.

"Hello, Gaspard."

Pure steel clanged in his voice.

Gaspard turned, blanched and then schooled his expression back to politeness. All in the space of a breath. "Dmitri."

The gazebo, which she had thought lovely seconds ago, suddenly felt like a battleground. Why did Dmitri look like he had seen a ghost?

He took another step, his gaze lingering on Gaspard's

hand over hers. "I see that you're already hovering around Jas like a vulture."

"Jas?" the man said, flicking his gaze between her and Dmitri. His nose flared as if he was a hyena scenting something. "But Ms. Douglas has been regaling me with tales of where she grew up…" He looked at Jasmine again, lingering on her diamond pendant and her dress. His brow cleared. The conclusion he so obviously came to was like a slap to her senses. "Is she one of yours, then?"

"I'm not *anyone's*, Mr. Devue." Jasmine wanted to slap the man and then thump Dmitri. "Really, Dmitri, don't—"

Cutting her off, he clasped her wrist and pulled her roughly to his side.

She resisted, or tried to. As a result, she ended up being slammed against his side.

Her breath left her in a soft gasp, a hundred different sensations swarming at her.

His hip pressed into her belly, the hard ridge of his muscled thigh straddled her legs and his forearm knocked into her breasts. His body was like a hot, hard cage around her shuddering muscles and shivering skin.

Sharp, instantaneous, all-consuming need filled every nook and crevice.

All the while the infuriating man stared at Gaspard, his expression disturbingly menacing. His arm stayed around her waist. "Jas is a childhood friend of mine and is in Athens as my guest." At least he hadn't said she was his possession. "She's not without protection, Gaspard. Do not come anywhere near her."

"Why don't you let the lady decide?"

"Unlike the women you terrify, I have nothing to lose." There was not even a facade of civility in Dmitri now.

Something crawled to the surface in the man's face, Jasmine was sure, before he spoke again. Something that made her uneasy. "Leah has my information, Ms. Douglas, if you would like to see me."

With another dark glance at Dmitri, the man left.

Jasmine felt her face flame as she saw that a few people had noticed the exchange. Saw the tasteless conclusion that they immediately came to.

They thought she was Dmitri's mistress and Gaspard had been poaching.

Bile coated her throat. The entire evening fell apart, instantly became dirty to her in a way that was reminiscent of her old life.

She turned to Dmitri, clutching the fury that threatened to split her from the inside. "What is it with you? Are you so sadistic that not only will you humiliate me but you won't let another man talk to me?"

Instead of the infuriatingly calm expression she usually got, a tic played in his jaw. "You don't know that man. It's got nothing to do with what's going on between you and—"

"Stop, just stop."

She looked around, trying to recall the simple joy she had felt this evening when she had put the dress on, when she had looked at herself…when she had, despite her effort not to, imagined the look in his eyes.

"All I wanted was to spend one evening like a normal person. Just dance, meet a few people who don't know what or where I have come from and have fun. Without you and this whole spectacle between us hanging over my head. Without worrying about the past or tomorrow. Now you have made me into an object of speculation. You made me feel as dirty as I have always believed myself to be."

His silence only lent weight to her accusation.

"I'm going to go over there and apologize to Gaspard. Stay away from me, *please*. The last thing I want is to create a scene at Leah and Stavros's wedding after intruding on it so shamelessly in the first place."

His fingers clamped over her wrist like a vise. "No, you'll not. You don't need to apologize to—"

"No, what I don't need is you in my life, even for another second. What I don't need is you dragging me around and dumping me without a word, leaving me to wonder what I'm going to do the next day. What I don't need is for you to make me feel as though every decision I have ever made is wrong, as if my entire life is one giant mistake.

"*God*, I'm so stupid I kept making excuses for you. I kept thinking…

"No wonder Andrew didn't want anything to do with you. No wonder he told me again and again that we were better off without you."

His skin pulled taut over his bones, his mouth blanching at her reckless words. "You're wrong, about everything."

CHAPTER EIGHT

SHE HAD JUST reached her room when Dmitri barged into the room. The thud of the door as he closed it with his shoulder sank into Jas's bones.

He flung the dinner jacket away, untied the buttons of his shirt. Was he preparing for a fight instead of walking away as usual? she wondered. Even that little bit of attention gathered momentum inside her.

God, she had it bad.

She leaned her forehead against the dark wood paneling of the wardrobe and closed her eyes. "I don't want to look at you…"

"No. I won't let you sneak away. Not until you hear me out."

"That's the problem with you, Dmitri," she said, still stunned at his mutinous tone.

Now he cared what she thought of him, that he had made her angry? That he had hurt her? Why?

"I have made it by myself all these years. Until you… stop treating me as if I'm rubbish you have been forced to rescue by a thin thread of conscience that you can't rid yourself of, I have nothing to say to you. Nor do I wish to listen to anything you might have to say."

They watched each other for an eternity of seconds. How was it that all her self-worth seemed to hinge on what Dmitri thought of her or how he talked to her? Or how he kissed her?

Was it a genetic trait that her mom had passed on to her, this eternal fixation on one man?

And slowly, sinuously, as if it was a snake waiting to strike, that awareness pulsed into life. Jasmine looked away to beat it back. The luxuriously soft red duvet covering the huge antique four-poster bed stared back at her, and the fever in her blood multiplied.

His arm stretched toward his nape, he finally spoke. "I have never thought of you as rubbish."

His deceptively flat statement lay in the space between them. Molten gray eyes challenging her to take it up, and hers surely reflecting her panic...

Her struggle lasted all of two seconds, that *same something* inside her being pulled toward him. As it had always been. "All your actions say otherwise."

"I was so angry that I could have wrung your neck for not coming to me sooner, yes. But I didn't think that of you, not once."

She could see him measuring his words now. What had changed?

Before she could argue, he held up a hand. "I didn't realize that leaving you in the middle of the night could be construed as—"

"Hurtful? Insensitive? It wasn't the point you were exactly trying to make?"

"No. I just couldn't wait to..."

"To go back to whoever was waiting for you, I know." She thought she might be a little sick. "I shouldn't have kissed you like that, not when—"

"No, you shouldn't have. And I don't have a girlfriend."

Something tight relented in her chest and she blew out a breath. Just because she lost the little sense she had when she was near didn't mean Dmitri had to reciprocate. "I only realized this morning how much of your plans I wrecked. I didn't know that Leah insisted that you make me your plus one. I'm absolutely okay with sitting with the guests. Dmitri, are you listening?"

"You have been thinking about this a lot."

She commanded herself to not flush. The traitor that her body was, it continued, as it wanted. "This isn't even your house and you dump me here in the middle of the night, not to mention two nights before the wedding. If Leah hadn't—"

"I knew Leah would look after you. And this is my house," he drawled. "Not that it was still okay," he added when she glared.

Her mouth fell open in an O. "I thought it was Leah's grandfather's estate."

"Giannis was fair to his last breath. According to him, Stavros got Leah and consequently a bigger share in the company, so I got the estate."

"So you got the bad end of the deal, then?" she couldn't help pointing out.

Leaning against the traditional, four-poster bed, he laughed. All Jas could think was that they were in a small room with a huge bed and… "Only you and Stavros think Leah is worth more than a thousand-acre estate."

"You're like a greedy dragon that hoards treasure. How much is enough, Dmitri? Have you really become that shallow?"

"It enabled me to buy you, Jas, didn't it?" he said, and then looked away, as if he had said too much.

And Jas scrambled for something to say, something to fight her body's feverish reaction to him. "I get that you have your own life and that I pushed my way into it. I just… Just don't dump me on someone else. Once we figure out some kind of plan for my future, I won't bother you again."

"I've decided that you're not bothering me anymore," he said, in an arrogant tone that said he had decided a lot more things than that.

What the hell did that even mean?

That was a complete one-eighty, if she'd ever heard one. She didn't dare ask him what had caused this. Because she was terrified he would tell her that he'd moved from mild annoyance to pity, that it was something from his past that had fractured through that facade tonight and not her...that she would realize that when it came to him, she would take anything.

God, she couldn't catch her breath with this man.

"But what you did just now, that was not okay on any level. You humiliated me. It's as though you really think I'm one of your possessions."

"Possession, Jas?" A winter storm blazed in his eyes. "You froze like a deer caught in headlights when he touched you."

"Dmitri, I'm not completely clueless when it comes to men. I know how—"

"Gaspard Devue is the worst kind of man, Jas." He reached her and Jasmine forgot how to breathe. He took her hand in his and looked down at them. Hers, slender and soft, his dark and rough—it was so...simply sexy. "That he gets to roam free like that after everything he keeps doing... I don't think Leah knows what kind of a man he is or she would have never let him step foot here. When I saw his hands on you, bile crawled up my throat.

"He has these toxic relationships with women. He abuses them in ways that I can't even bear to think of. I have seen his handiwork on Anya and—"

"Anya Ivanova, the supermodel? The one you were going to marry?" she piped up. Then wanted to sink through the floor when his mouth tensed.

He stared at her for a long time before he nodded. "He isolated her, beat her and, when she threatened to tell the authorities, he pulled the rug out from under her life by spreading vicious rumors about her work. Terrified to within an inch of her life, she came to me. I offered to stay with her at an Alps resort while she recovered. But however much I reassured her, she refused to press charges."

And the gossip magazines had thought a woman had finally conquered Dmitri Karegas. Dark and light, they had complemented each other perfectly. Jasmine had bought the tabloid, read it through and then ripped it into shreds, and had stood shaken by the depth of her envy for a woman she knew nothing about.

While he had been helping an abused woman recover her life.

Jasmine had a feeling she was seeing a side of Dmitri no one did. Except the unfortunate woman.

"Gaspard was the one who found her in St. Petersburg when she was barely seventeen, gave her her first big break. And through the years, he isolated her, abused her. Until she thought there was nowhere else to go, caught in that relationship."

And Dmitri had got her out of it. "She quit modeling, didn't she?"

"Yes, I helped her get out of some of the contracts." He shrugged.

When there had been no announcement of an engagement coming, the tabloids had gone berserk. Nothing had come out of it except Anya Ivanova, she suddenly remembered breathlessly, had started a retail clothes store in London.

With Dmitri's backing, Jasmine realized, the pieces falling into place. He had helped the woman get on her feet, but she knew he wouldn't mention that.

Just like he wouldn't mention anything that betrayed the man he was beneath the facade. She understood now why he had reacted so violently, saw the shadows of the past fill his eyes.

"I saw that flicker of interest in his eyes when he looked

at you. If he so much as comes anywhere near you again, I will..." The barely restrained violence in him would have scared her if she hadn't known him once.

If he could do so much for an ex, Jas wasn't surprised at what he had done for her. After all, he had admitted that he owed Andrew. For all his playboy persona, Dmitri seemed to have a white-knight complex.

And she had been nothing but a literal damsel.

"Promise me that you will stay away from such men in the future."

"Isn't seeing him a long way from falling into an abusive relationship, Dmitri?"

"It is, but I..."

She gasped as realization sunk in.

He thought she was ripe for picking for a man like Gaspard, that she had no sense of self-preservation at all. Or maybe he thought she was like her mother.

But then, ever since she had come into his life, all she had done was act like a pushover. It didn't help to know that it was only he who made her act so out of character. "You think I'm more prone to it?"

"*Theos*, Jas, I don't want to argue with you. Just give me your word."

"I won't see him," Jasmine said first, wanting more than anything to reassure him. As to what the man's actual offer had been, she had no idea, but she didn't mention that to Dmitri. She sighed. "Believe it or not, I wouldn't have blithely gone off with Gaspard tonight or any other night. You give me far less credit. I made hard, gut-wrenching choices, but I did survive on my own, Dmitri."

"You have no idea how sorry I am about that."

"Why?" She shook her head. "It is not your fault."

And just like that she accepted it wasn't. When she had asked for help, he had come, guns blazing. What more could she ask for?

That they had grown apart was nothing but a circumstance of their lives. That she had held on to the memory of him all these years… It was an affliction she needed to grow out of.

"Partly it is. I…should have taken on your responsibility at Andrew's funeral, should have made some kind of arrangement for your future."

"Stop saying that. I never wanted you to fix my life, Dmitri. I just…needed a friend. Andrew needed a friend."

A growl fell from his mouth, a jagged sound of frustration and regret. "I should have known what Andrew would do. I should have…never trusted him. I should have…"

What did he mean? Fear fisted tight in her gut.

"Tell me to walk away, Jas," he said in that controlled voice that she was beginning to hate. "Tell me to leave the past where it should be. Tell me to hang on to the little honor I have."

He looked so painfully handsome, so achingly real. And she was terrified of asking but equally of not knowing… She felt as though she was standing at a precipice that she had been trying to reach all her life, as though the real Dmitri was finally within her reach.

"What did you mean by that?"

He knelt in front of her and a flutter began in Jasmine's belly. Tilted upward toward her, he reached for her and Jasmine started shivering. Warm, rough hands clasped her bare shoulders. "You're cold?"

"No. It's you," she whispered, knowing that there was nothing to hide from his gaze.

Fragile, she felt so fragile when he touched her like that…

His fingers lifted her pendant off her skin, the tips brushing against the curve of her breast. She closed her eyes, sharp tingles taking over her body. "I should have got the matching earrings, too."

A storm unleashed in her gut as the words fell over her.

Snatching away the pendant from his fingers, she looked up. "Wait…you were the one who had it delivered for my eighteenth birthday? But that's impossible. Why would Andrew say he had ordered it?"

The truth slammed into her from every which way, shaking the very axis of her life.

"Because he lied to you and to me. He told me you were better off without me in your life and I believed him. And I didn't care who you thought it was from as long as you had it."

It was all there in his eyes—the guilt, the pain, the lies he had allowed her to believe. He didn't have to say a word. And in that minute, she saw what she had been too blind to see.

"You came back to see us… Oh, God… When, how?"

He ran a hand through his hair. "That first year, I ran away three times and almost reached London. But Stavros just kept getting better and better at stopping me. Finally, Giannis made a deal with me. If I met every challenge he had for me, he would bring me himself to see Andrew. And I did. I worked round the clock. I begged Stavros to teach me everything he knew. I began to control my temper… And the little money I made in those first couple of years, which was truly nothing, I gave to Andrew."

She didn't care if it might have been nothing. He had been given a new lease on life, a life none of them had ever dreamed of, and he still had come back for them.

"You gave him money…" She slid onto the bench at the foot of the bed soundlessly, the whole picture emerging in front of her. Her gut turned so painfully that she thought she might be sick. "For how long?"

"Years."

Shock shattered her, bringing shards of pain with it.

"When I realized what he'd been doing, when his words

didn't add up anymore, I cut him off instantly. But his addiction to gambling was already in his bones. I should have realized he would somehow find the money, that the burden would fall to you. He had already turned you against me, and after he was gone…there was no point in telling you the truth."

He had protected Andrew even then. *And her from the ugly truth.* For a man who said he had done everything only to alleviate guilt, Dmitri had done so much for them.

More than their own mother.

"The last time he came to see me, I begged him to tell me where you were. And he said he would if I gave him money." He pressed his palms to his eyes. "It was the hardest thing to see him like that…"

"He made me hate you." God, Andrew had not only squandered what Dmitri gave him but borrowed more from Noah… "I'm so sorry…for all the things I said to you. For what he did."

Dmitri crouched in front of her, his long fingers stroking over her bare arms. She shivered, and pressed her forehead in his shoulder. Shame and grief vied for space within her. "Don't, Jas. You've carried his burden long enough."

His hands moved over her shoulders and soon she was in his embrace.

Jasmine wished she could cry and let it all out. But fury had turned into a hard knot and settled deep in her chest. She felt like ice.

Andrew had cheated both her and Dmitri to the very end.

That addiction was in their genes, their blood. And she was just as prone to it as they had been. Did hers come in the form of this man? Was it already too late?

But Jasmine found she couldn't care. She didn't care.

Her brother's betrayal cut too deep. All those years of slaving herself over a debt he had made, of defending him in her own mind, of putting her barely clothed body on display every night—all of it had been for nothing. The grief that she hadn't somehow been enough to get him through it… The crushing weight lifted.

She had paid the price for their weaknesses, their addictions. She would pay no more, not in shame, not in grief, and not by making their weaknesses her own.

The ice cracked just like that, the white-hot flame of her fury, her powerlessness found target in the man in front of her.

She jerked away from him. "Why did you tell me all this today? Why not that first night? Why now?"

Something desperate flashed in his eyes when he spoke. "You wish I hadn't told you?"

"No, I want to know what changed today."

Suddenly, she understood the second layer to his reaction when Gaspard had touched her.

She remembered the carnal promise in that blinding, incinerating moment on the flight when he had devoured her mouth, as if he was drowning. Finally, she understood what Dmitri had been hiding since the first night beneath his lacerating contempt for her…

An avalanche of want and need ripped open inside her as she looked at him with new eyes… He had wanted her all along… Then, why had he pushed her away so efficiently?

"Tell me, Dmitri," she commanded now, fully aware of what she was asking. No longer confused about her own want for him, no longer guilty or ashamed about it.

She'd never been an innocent, except in the most technical sense anyway.

Still, he had given her a choice.

She wanted him; she had known that from the beginning. But tonight, there was no shame or weakness that came with that want. Tonight there was nothing but the two of them.

"Because I realized the inevitability of this thing between us." His soft voice only amplified the spiraling tension in the room. "If not today, tomorrow. If not tomorrow… It's going to consume us both.

"I have never denied myself something I want. I want you. Every time you look at me, all I can think of is being inside you. Every time you lash at me, all I can think of is kissing your mouth… To hell with your debt and my honor, and Andrew… To hell with pretending I'm something I'm not. Nothing in the past decade has made me as hungry or as desperate as you have, Jas. So do you want this for as long as it will last? Do you have the guts to actually take me on, Jas? Because if I touch you, I won't stop."

For a seemingly infinite moment, she looked as though she would tell him to go to the farthest corners of hell. *Theos*, he deserved it just for the way he had treated her this past week. He already had a one-way ticket there for what he was about to do.

He was going to slake his lust and move on… Because that was all he did. That was all he had ever been capable of.

But he was through with being something he was not. He was through with denying himself. And he didn't allow himself to think of the consequences tomorrow. He'd deal with it.

Right now all he wanted was to taste that lush mouth again, remove that hurt from her eyes.

"You were attracted to me all along?" she demanded.

The gold fabric molding her lithe body, she looked like a goddess who had only just realized her power.

His heart threatened to shove past his rib cage. "*Attraction* is such a lukewarm word, *pethi mou*."

Even in that desperate last moment, he had tried for honor, Dmitri told himself. He had sounded nothing like a lover should. *Christos*, he was more tender with women whose name he didn't know, but with her, he sounded like an arrogant, lust-riddled jerk.

But at least he had told her what his terms were. If she didn't want him like that, she could walk away.

He was not seducing her, he told himself.

And then suddenly, she was walking toward him, and he shuddered with relief and tension and anticipation.

Before his next breath, her hands were in his hair and pulling his head down to meet her mouth. They groaned and pressed closer to each other, as if they couldn't get enough already.

He took her mouth with desperation and rough need, swiping at her trembling mouth with his tongue, impatient to possess her. And she...she was draped around him like ivy, her breasts rubbing and pressing his chest, one long leg wrapped around his as she moaned.

And the last flicker of self-restraint he possessed went out.

The taste of her had clung to him for two days, her jagged whimpers etched on his brain. Never had a woman so thoroughly consumed his every thought, never had she felt so out of his reach... He didn't question the possessive fire he felt as he learned her.

He had already decided when it came to Jasmine, he was mad.

Dmitri ran his hands over the taut line of her back to her rounded buttocks, the narrow flare of her hips. There were so many places to touch, so many places to learn. And she sank into his rough caresses, gasping and moaning under his mouth. As if she was as out of control for him as he was for her.

He dipped his hands into her hair and molded her scalp,

bending her to his plundering mouth. Like raw silk, her hair cascaded through his fingers. She smelled of wild-flowers and summer, and he breathed it in, hungry for every texture of her.

The more he touched her and stroked her and tasted her, the smooth forehead, the narrow bridge of her nose, the already red curve of her mouth, the pulse that skittered at her neck, the rim of her dainty ears, the more he thought of someone else's hands on all of it...on all of her...

Of someone, scum like Gaspard or John King or someone like his father, laying a finger on her, marring skin that was like satin, touching curves that were pure perfection, forever ruining that innocent yet wild spirit inside her, the hotter his anger and desire burned...

He took and took, licked and bit, stroked and tasted, plundered and devoured her mouth until she was panting and moaning, and gasping his name...

"Dmitri..." she whispered against his bristly jaw.

The trailing heat of her mouth against his neck made his throat dry. He pulled her up again, afraid that he would ravage her if she so much as kissed his skin...

Then she said it again, his name.

It fell from her mouth like a warm caress, an entreaty and command all wrapped in one... Hearing his name on her lips did what the little will he had over his body couldn't... It calmed him down, called him down from the edge.

He couldn't take her like every other woman in the world, not because of her innocence, but this was her...

"Keep saying my name like that," he commanded, looking for a hook, or a zipper, something that would reveal her to him.

Her arms around his nape, her mouth against his, she complied. *"Dmitri."*

Too impatient now to think straight, he caught the crisscrossing strips of the gold silk and pushed it down her shoulders. Not before running the back of his hands over the hard nipples visible through the silk.

She made a sound, like a throaty purr, at the back of her throat, her gaze unabashedly meeting his. The liquid longing he saw there threatened to undo him.

The dress slithered down her breasts and hips with a silky whisper and pooled around her legs.

Dmitri stepped back, the better to see her, his breath knocking about in his throat. And almost lost it then.

It felt as though he had waited forever to see Jasmine like this and hadn't even known it.

He lost all sense of himself and time and space as he took in the glory of her body.

For a woman who'd never been with a man, she didn't slouch or cover her breasts, or bend her knees. Her slender shoulders thrown back, she stared back at him. Only her fluttering lashes and the tremble in her mouth betrayed her struggle.

Something feverish burned in her dark gaze, a gauntlet thrown. As if she was daring him to find fault with her now, to insult her again with his words.

Her breasts were lush and firm, with plump nipples that grew tight under his hungry gaze. His mouth went dry, his breath came in panting gasps as he drank in more and more of her. The flat plane of her stomach, the small tattoo, a rose, just above her bikini line and the shadow of the dark hair covering her sex underneath the sheer skin-colored thong.

Slowly, softly, as if she had done the same thing a million times, as if it was etched into her DNA, she stepped out of the pool of the dress and kicked it with a flick of her foot.

Three-inch stilettos with strings wrapped around her ankles, her long, sleek, toned legs completed the picture.

Somewhere in the past few seconds, his erection went from hard to painful, contained in his boxers. He had never been brought to such arousal just by looking at a woman. If she so much as touched him…

All the while his brain grappled to keep enough blood to form a coherent thought.

Something didn't add up, it said before his libido took over again.

But, drowning in desire, Dmitri found he didn't care.

All he wanted was to bury himself in her so deep that he never had to think again. That she forgot to breathe. "Take off the thong," he ordered, his throat croaking to form the words.

"And the heels?" she threw back, sounding husky and breathless, and he thought he would implode.

It was as if a different woman had emerged when she took off her clothes. No matter, he told himself, pushing himself off his feet.

He would learn every facet there was of Jasmine, every inch of her; every thought that passed her mind would all be his soon.

There would be nothing left of her that he didn't know, touch or taste.

"Keep them on," he said, determined to unravel her just as thoroughly as she had done him from the moment she had come at him with that damned knife.

It was as if with that one strike, she had permanently etched herself into his skin.

CHAPTER NINE

JASMINE WAS FINALLY, incontrovertibly ready to be the woman she wanted to be. She was ready to be just her, devoid of ghosts from the past, ready to own her pleasure, her life.

Clasping her nape with one hand, he caressed her hip with the other. Chest to breasts, hip to hip, thigh to thigh, they stood flush against each other. His erection, a searing brand against her lower belly, lengthened, and the thought of him inside her filled her with a mixture of excitement and anticipation. "It's going to hurt whatever I do," he whispered against her mouth. "I can't change that."

Something more than simple pleasure billowed in her chest that he respected her enough to tell the truth. That he didn't cover it up. That there was finally truth between them, at least in this.

"I don't care." She met his eyes squarely. "I'm not the girl you saved, not the sister of the man you owed a debt to, not the girl you feel sorry for. I'm just me tonight, Dmitri, and I have waited so long to feel like this... And I want the real you. Not tenderness that you have to fabricate, not lies you use to tether me, just you."

"You'll be the end of me."

She smiled, shivering from head to toe. "Then, I hope it's a pleasurable end."

Fisting his hand in her hair, Dmitri took her mouth in a bruising kiss. This kiss was hotter and harder than ever before, his tongue plunging into her mouth mercilessly. She could feel herself getting wet, the chafing of her thong too much to bear.

Her breasts pressed against his, his other hand splayed big and hard over her bare butt. "*Theos*, you're made for this, your body... I've never seen anything sexier."

Jasmine shuddered violently, pleasure shooting across and over her, like molten metal flowing into all the places she had hidden even from herself. Her body had been nothing but an instrument for survival until now, something she had detested, something she had centered her shame on.

Dmitri's words and caresses made her love it as much as he seemed to, freed her from her own shackles.

He pushed her against the wall, his suit-clad thigh jammed between hers, rubbing against her heated core. Pulling her hands above her head, he held them there.

The fiercely possessive heat in his eyes sent her insides swooping as if she was on a downward fall.

He trailed those sexy lips over her cheek, her jaw, licked the rim of her ear and then traced it down to the pulse at her neck. Throwing her head back, she gave in to it. This was what she wanted—Dmitri in all his bad-boy glory.

When his mouth closed over her pulse, Jasmine shuddered, hard. She had been terrified that he would be gentle with her, that he would be that fake, sophisticated version of him. But he was not, and her heart soared at that.

He was in this moment as fully as she had been, as real as he had been to her all those years ago.

Her stomach curled in delicious spasms as he dragged his mouth down, over the valley between her breasts. While one hand still arrested her hands from touching him, he palmed her breast with the other. Lifted the firm weight to his mouth and flicked the tight bud with his wicked tongue. Jasmine arched into him in mindless need.

Sensations sparked all over her, leaving little shivers in their wake.

Holding her hard against the wall with one shoulder while his white-hot gaze consumed her, he took the hard nipple into his mouth and sucked.

She came off the wall like an arrow, pleasure shooting down between her thighs. Her body felt like one pulsing mass of pleasure as he continued the torment with his tongue and, *oh, dear*, his teeth.

At some point, Jasmine stopped fighting and began sobbing and moaning and begging. His name became her mantra as he continued his relentless assault.

She had thought she knew what lust meant, what incited it. Thought it dirty. Despised how willingly one took on such intimacy for a few moments of pleasure, had thought the whole world crazy...

But the intimacy of their heated looks, the shared breaths, the fact his desire for her finally revealed the real Dmitri to her was just as arousing as the pleasure he was drenching her in.

There was not an inch of skin he didn't kiss or taste or suck. An intolerable, insistent ache built in her lower belly.

She sank her hands into his hair as he kissed his way down her abdomen, his willing slave. He was still in the snowy white dress shirt and trousers while she was naked and that, too, felt erotic, that, too, was intended to remind her that he was bending her very body, her will to his.

But she didn't care. All she wanted was to go wherever he took her, revel in whatever he gave her. To be possessed by him in every way that mattered.

And then he was kneeling in front of her, his face pressed to the flimsy triangle of fabric that covered her sex. "*Theos*, I can't wait to taste you, Jas."

She was flushing and panting, and moaning...as he rolled down the thong and lifted her leg.

Jasmine became boneless as he threw one leg over his shoulder, his harsh breath fluttering over the sensitive skin of her inner thighs. Thought she would melt into a puddle on the floor if he didn't hold her up with an arm against her soft belly.

"Oh…" The word floated out of her mouth.

When the first flick of his tongue came over her wet folds, it was as if someone had plunged a knife from her spine to her belly, so sharp and acute was the sensation.

Then he did it again, dipping that wicked tongue into her wet warmth with such expertise that she wanted to die from the onslaught of pleasure.

She shifted and snarled against the wall as he continued licking her, the pressure relentlessly sending her up and up.

"Please, Dmitri…" she pleaded, unable to bear it anymore.

"Look down at me," he commanded in a raw whisper.

Her hands in his hair, Jas looked down. Kneeling in front of her, his mouth tucked against the most intimate part of her, he looked like some pagan god come to wreak havoc, and she his feast.

As she watched, caught in the languorous heat in his eyes, his mouth closed over the swollen, excruciatingly swollen bundle of nerves and pulled ever so gently.

She screamed his name as she shattered into a million shards, her hips bucking against his mouth, her lower belly still spasming violently. He kept on and on until every last drop of pleasure was wrenched from her body.

When her knees buckled, he caught her and lifted her into his arms.

He carried her to the bed, his gaze drinking in her face. She fell in an inelegant heap, her heart still not back to normal after the earth-shattering climax.

Only the moonlight from the veranda illuminated the room, music and voices floating up from the party. Even that intrusion was too much for Jas. She didn't want to share Dmitri for a second.

His gaze stayed on her with the same intense hunger, as if all he wanted to do was to drink in her nakedness. Skin tingling at his perusal, she watched him as he shed his shirt, his trousers and the black boxers. Then he was gloriously naked, all hard angles and masculine power.

His tight shoulders appeared first, and then that muscular chest of his, velvet skin delineated over ropes of muscles, a washboard stomach and then...

"Oh, wow," she whispered at the sight of his turgid shaft.

Color slashed those cheekbones but he didn't smile.

Stretching her arm, which took every ounce of strength she had, she ran a finger from the base all the way to the soft head. So many men had made passes at her, from such an early age, and she had hated them and herself... had tuned out any and all curiosity and interest in men as a rule, first because of her mum and then because of what she had been doing...

"I finally get why so many women go gaga over you," she said huskily, still in a haze from the orgasm. But she didn't want to hide or feel ashamed at what should be natural, didn't want to punish herself for mistakes she hadn't made. "Just looking at you fills me with all kinds of ideas."

"One forbidden indulgence at a time, *glykia mou*." He stepped closer to the bed, and pulled her to him. "And who knows, by tomorrow morning, we might be done with each other."

She was slowly learning him now. When he felt something deeply, which was more often than not despite his facade, that was when he used those cruel words, to better hide behind them. Or to bury what he felt. Or to lash out.

Would he run if he knew how much of herself she was

giving in this moment? How much she wanted her body to please him, how much she wanted to leave a mark on him?

How many of her own shackles he was releasing her from?

She slid closer to him on the soft sheets, came up on her knees and bent. Her hair cascaded around her, giving her a second to overcome the heat tightening her cheeks.

Because more than anything, she wanted to please him.

She brought the rigid shaft to her mouth and licked the length of him. Velvet tightness over steel in her hand, his taste exploded on her tongue.

His breath hissed out of him, his hands sinking into her hair. She did it again and for a few seconds, his fingers fisted in her hair, dug into her scalp and held her there.

That raw glimpse into his need sent power spiraling through her, as if she had been jolted with a burst of it. Wrapping her tingling mouth around the broad head, she closed her mouth around it and sucked on him.

His curse reverberated around the silent room, only fractured by his harsh breaths.

Like an earthquake's aftershock, a tremor went through her lower belly at the taste of him, at the raw-edged need in his guttural groan. Addicted to her own pleasure, she looked up at him and did it again.

When she fisted her hand around that hard length, he pushed her back against the bed, none too gently.

He climbed onto the bed and over her, like a conquering warrior looking at his spoils. Lying on his side, he pulled her trembling body closer to him, one muscular thigh locking her against the bed when she tried to wriggle out of his hold. "Enough playing, *thee mou*. I want to be inside you *now*."

His hands moved down her belly and into her folds, as if he didn't listen to his own rules.

Intrusive and intimate, his fingers parted her. She

twisted the sheets and moaned. But was determined to say her bit. "I want to return the pleasure you gave me," she whispered, desperate to keep the tension out of her voice.

Because now that the flush of her pleasure was fading, anxiety at what was to come ate through her. She wasn't worried about pain; it was a fact of life. But his words still rattled around at the back of her brain.

High maintenance... She would die if he didn't find pleasure with her...

His kiss came like a cinder again, firing off every nerve, just when she thought she would never recover again.

"You think you're not giving me pleasure, Jas *mou*?"

He covered her with his body and Jas lost track of what she was thinking again. "You scream as if you're falling apart, you kiss as if you can't breathe, you sink into every caress, *Theos*... I can't breathe for imagining all the ways, all the places I'm going to take you..."

A gasp exploded out of her mouth when he pushed first one, and then two fingers into her inviting warmth, all the while his thumb pressing against the bundle of nerves at her core.

Through a fog of lust, she heard his pithy curse about protection and stayed his hand. "I've been on the pill since I was sixteen. In that, my mother was the model of a responsible parent. Or maybe she thought I would be just as weak and desperate as her."

She closed her eyes, disgusted that the echo of fear and shame she had held on to for so long still could rattle through her.

He came back to her and kissed her temple with such tenderness that tears knocked at her eyes. "Look at me, Jas."

When she didn't comply, he kissed her eyelids, the tip of her nose and her mouth.

He parted her legs and settled between them, his hip bone digging deliciously into her thigh. "You're nothing like her, *agape mou*. Don't you already know that? Your fire—" he kissed the valley between her breasts "—your reckless courage—" his tongue flicked her navel "—your heat—" her tattoo got his kiss now "—and passion—" long and unbelievably hard, his shaft settled at her sex, teasing her "—and innocence and kindness."

The tip probed the entrance while his mouth closed over her nipple. New sparks of need broke into life and Jas moved under him, restless in her own skin again. Desperate to have him inside her, desperate to be his in that final way…

His hands held her hips with a bruising grip and Jas writhed as the velvet heat of him scorched her already sensitized sex. "You're all the things none of us ever was, Jas, neither me nor Andrew," he whispered against her skin. "You are simply perfection." Drunk on his words, she reached for him just as he thrust into her in one smooth, sure stroke.

A curse ripped from his mouth just as pain cleaved through her pelvis.

Jas became rigid under him, her nails gouging his back, trying to get him to still, trying to breathe through the alien and achy and full feeling of having him inside her.

Dmitri was inside her, the wanton, willing part of her was screaming in her head. Magnificently masculine, he was heat and steel and hard around her and inside her, and there wasn't even a single breath she could take that didn't bring more awareness of him into her. She dug her teeth into his shoulder, tasted salt and sweat and him.

"You're doing beautifully, Jas." Drugged, his words rumbled against her rib cage. "You're… *Thee mou*, you feel like heaven."

Large, rough hands held her shoulders down and then

he thrust again, and he was now as thoroughly lodged inside her as he was lodged under her skin, in her heart.

A gasp tore from her mouth, borne more out of a new fire than discomfort.

His chest rasped against her breasts as he said something in Greek, but the pinch of pain was already receding and Jas was floating because even though she didn't understand what he had muttered, she did know that he was in an agony of pleasure, devoid of his control, shuddering in the wake of it just as she was.

Clasping his jaw, she pulled his head down so that she could look into his eyes. So that he knew it was she as irrevocably as she knew it was him. "Does it feel good, Dmitri?" she asked, determined to know for sure.

A series of curse words fell from his mouth, one filthier than the previous and Jas found herself smiling, her heart stuttering with joy. He pushed back her hair from her damp forehead gently. "That's for me to ask, *agape mou*. How do you feel?"

"As if I will die if you move and die anyway if you don't." A fierce heat began to build up her chest as he played idly with her nipple. The tip puckered at his touch, knotting and sending a pulse of sensation to her pelvis. "Tell me, Dmitri, how does it feel for you?" She dragged at his lower lip with her teeth and he hissed in response. "The truth, if you please."

Softly, slowly, he kissed her shoulder and she felt his damp forehead. She had a feeling that he was cooling himself down, like a wild animal catching a breath, before continuing the hunt. "You're so tight and hot and I'm too aroused and hard…" He rested his dark head between her breasts and expelled a sharp breath, the blade of his shoulders rattling visibly. "Jas, I can't change it and I can't change how good it feels to me while… I've never given anything, true, but I don't want to rain hurt on you, either."

He sounded so unlike himself that Jas smiled. And the man thought he didn't have tenderness in him. "But it doesn't anymore."

She dug her fingers into his taut buttocks and squeezed in closer, anchored herself on his rock-hard thighs. The hair on his thighs rasped against her palms; the leashed power in his body made everything thrum. She couldn't get enough of him, couldn't get enough of what he was doing to her. Couldn't breathe when she imagined all the things he could do to her with that powerful body, couldn't breathe at how fragile and delicate and precious she felt trapped under him. "And I trust you to make it better."

Tangling her hands in his hair, she took his mouth in a soft kiss that soon morphed into something else.

He met her gaze. He was incredibly still, almost crushing her into the mattress but he was gorgeous. "I can't go slow. You're incredibly wet and hot and I…just don't have it in me to be… I'm a selfish man, Jas."

"Selfish man who just made me see the stars and the sky? You're not too bad, Dmitri. And believe me, I won't break."

And to prove it to him, she thrust up experimentally. His hands on her hips holding her down, he withdrew almost all the way and then thrust back in.

Jasmine was in heaven or hell or someplace in between as he moved in and out with slow, measured thrusts that seemed to be for the express purpose of driving her out of her skin. "Faster, please," she said, and when he didn't oblige, she bit his shoulder.

The pace of his thrusts became faster, more desperate, less measured, one hand on her hip and one in her hair, his tight grip adding an edge of pain to the scorching pleasure.

The faster and rougher he got, the hotter and higher she climbed, his swift strokes wrenching arousal from her again.

Just for a second, he paused and sneaked his fingers between them and pressed down. And she fell apart. He took up his rhythm again as she came, his face a study in passion and need.

This time she didn't close her eyes.

She didn't want to miss the intensity of his passion, the gray fire in his eyes, the tightness of every feature, the corded stillness of his shoulder blades, the tiny beads of sweat along his upper lip, the growl that fell from his mouth as he pumped into her one last time and collapsed over her.

Wrapping her hands around him, Jasmine bore his crushing weight willingly.

She was now irrevocably a woman. And she liked all the perks that came with it. And the man who had taken her there with such an all-consuming passion, the man who claimed to possess no tenderness and did no emotions, who took on blame for her brother's sins, who made an art of the mask he showed the world... She was falling fast for him.

But whether it was the postcoital haze or the happy hormones their session of lovemaking filled her with, Jasmine couldn't care.

CHAPTER TEN

DMITRI PULLED JAS with him as he lay back on the bed. The echo of his release still pumped aftershocks through him, a climax that had been as emotional as it had been intense.

Her dares and her questions, the pleasure and pain and joy in her eyes... It wasn't just her body she had shared with him. Just like the little girl she had been, Jasmine gave whatever she had with generosity, felt everything she did with a sharp hunger that was so incredibly beautiful to watch...

For the first time in his life, sex for him hadn't been just about animal release but connection and intimacy, about kisses and sweet promises, about give and take of more than just release.

It was impossible to make love to Jas without taking a part of her.

Without a part of him wrenching away from him whether he willed it or not.

He had never felt this satisfaction, the visceral rightness of what had happened. This...sense of joy at a woman draped over him with such possessive pleasure. It went bone deep and he felt absolutely no inclination to get up and move, even though he usually headed directly to the shower after sex.

Her skin was damp to his touch, her breaths coming in panting pulls against his shoulder. Delicate fingers spread out over his chest, she kept her eyes closed.

She looked and felt perfect against the length of him, her hair spilling over his forearm.

He pulled the duvet up to cover them, his mouth going dry at the sight of her round buttocks, the flare of her hip. Still her breasts were flush against his side, and the thought of rolling those plump nipples on his tongue made him hard again.

"You are fine?" His voice came out gruff and growly.

Without opening her eyes, she nodded. Her hand moved restlessly over his chest, traced the ridges of his abdomen, came to rest on his shaft, over the duvet. He clasped her wrist, but she slapped him away and resumed her position. Heat punched through him as she played with it, a soft smile playing around her lips.

As if it was her right to fondle him. As if there was nothing else she would rather do.

"Jas, if you keep doing that, I will take you again."

Her mouth pressed into his skin. "So who's stopping you?"

Something between a groan and a growl escaped him as she pushed herself upon her elbow and proceeded to lick his nipple. As though she were a cat and he cream. "Your body is unused to this, *to me*. Since you don't seem to possess any good sense, it falls to me. And I'd rather not test my self-control, especially when it comes to you."

"Okay," she agreed, and moved her hand up to his chest but showed no signs of releasing him.

Theos, he hadn't meant to say so much.

Did he have to spell out everything to the infuriating woman? Did she find some perverse pleasure in behaving so outrageously that he inevitably watched over her?

And beneath his increasing fervor to have her again, he found that he liked indulging Jasmine. He wanted to stay there and let her play with him, to see a smile light up her eyes.

Usually, he couldn't wait to get away the moment his release hit. He had tried a couple of times to stay, to wrench some kind of feeling out of himself but all he had felt was coldness, an instant detachment that curdled any pleasure he had found just minutes ago.

An empty hollowness that he couldn't rid himself of.

So he moved on, to the next chase, to the next warm body that would provide that ephemeral release.

And yet, languorous heat pumped through him as she caressed him with more of an artless curiosity rather than skilled strokes designed to arouse. With her vined around him like that, he never wanted to get out of the bed.

Dmitri knew he should feel guilty. Or some other horrible emotion should be coursing through him, remonstrating with him for his lack of tenderness or finesse. Or shame that he had willingly given up that thread of honor Giannis had tried to instill in him.

Stavros would tell him, in that forbiddingly arrogant voice of his, that he should feel guilty about not feeling guilty, at least.

Breathing in the wild scent of Jas and sex combined, feeling her soft curves surround him, he couldn't bring himself to feel anything but the most primal kind of satisfaction.

Sated after the most intense sex of his life, he couldn't hate himself for it.

How could he when he barely ever felt anything this deep? When even the faces of the women he'd slept with the previous night faded by the next morning? When, sometimes, even sex didn't fill the void inside him for a few minutes?

The whole world, including Giannis, even Stavros, who knew him better than anyone else, thought he had no discipline, barely any self-control. That he gave in to every self-indulgence because that was all he cared about—pleasure and wealth and everything superficial.

What they didn't know was his inability to feel anything.

Not after he had cleaved himself in two and removed the guilt of his mother's death and the pain his father's fists had wreaked on him. That if he accessed anything deep, if he stayed too long with any woman or in any relationship, he started to panic.

As if that boy was just waiting to come back to life, bringing with him unbearable agony and pain. So he kept his entire life about casual relationships, transient fun. If not for Giannis first, and then Stavros grounding him, he had a feeling he would have become nothing but an empty shell who fed on transient pleasures and swam through life without meaning.

Until Jas had come into his life.

Her eyelids were drooping, and she still had that silly smile over her face. Then he was smiling because she looked infinitely breathtaking in the utter enthusiasm with which she'd embraced tonight.

And that smile knocked over into his life, kicking everything he had ever believed about himself wide-open, as though she was the domino who started it all. Digging his hands into her hair, he pulled her closer. "Why are you still smiling?"

Finally, she deigned to open her eyes and he found himself falling deeper and deeper into her spell. The openness of her expression made it impossible to be anything but. She looked at him as if he was the most wonderful thing she had ever seen.

It filled him with a strangely exhilarating weight that he had not known in his adult life. It magnified inside him, spreading to his chest, filling every nook and cranny. As if he was now responsible for keeping that smile on her face.

Her fingers found his mouth and traced the seam with

such a possessive touch. Expelling a harsh breath, he forced himself to relax. He never invited the woman he slept with to touch him, never lingered in the moment after seeing to their pleasure and his own. "Because it was *that* good." Her long lashes cast shadows over her cheeks as she struggled to keep her eyes open. "Tomorrow, I swear, Dmitri, you can have whatever you want," she offered magnanimously, as if she was a goddess granting boons.

He wanted to tell her she had already given him something precious—her trust. But he kept the words to himself. "You can, instead, answer my question now," he said, wondering anew at how at ease she had been with her body.

Theos, the woman was like a sensual missile, and thinking that about her made him think of her with other men and right now, he didn't want to go there.

It seemed being in bed with Jas meant every thought he had left him feeling either raw or uncertain or both.

"What?" she said, suddenly tense.

"What did you do all these years at Noah's nightclub, Jas?"

His heart hammered at her continued silence. Propping himself up, he looked at her.

Her shoulders became a rigid line, her gaze not meeting his as she pulled up the duvet to cover herself up.

"Jas, whatever it is—"

"I was a pole dancer in his underground nightclub."

While Dmitri grappled with that, she met his eyes. Full of fake defiance and shadows of shame, her gaze did nothing to abate the rage building inside him. "A pole dancer?" he repeated, disbelief and fury and guilt all rolling into his tone.

"I jumped in only because one of the girls was sick one day and was terrified of losing the spot. I told myself it was just for one night. Apparently, awful as I was that first night, I was still a huge hit. Guess I owe it to my fa-

ther for his contribution toward making me look *exotic*."
Loathing spewed out when she said that word. As if she
hated that about her and what it had enabled her to do.

"But the tips, Dmitri, they were ten times what I got
waitressing. Suddenly, I could at least dream of leaving
that life. I could imagine a different one." Her voice became small; her entire body scrunched into herself.

Shame, Dmitri realized slowly—that emotion in her
voice was shame. Was that why she had hidden the truth
from him until now? Why she thought she was beneath
him?

If only she knew his roots…

"So I practiced until my legs felt as if they would fall
off, until the heretofore unused muscles in my thighs and
calves burned as though there were knives lodged inside
them, put on mere scraps of lace and took to the stage. I
tuned out every man who looked at me as if I was a mor-
sel of meat instead of a woman with wants and fears, I
loathed myself a thousand times for every night I went
up there, but I did it.

"I was an instant super hit."

He blinked to clear the haze of red that covered his vi-
sion. "So what did Noah threaten you with that you came
to me finally?"

She flinched, her gaze shying away from him again.
"In the past year, I went from the side to center stage, and
the show went from a huge floor show to an outrageously
expensive, custom show.

"Suddenly, the men I'd tuned out all along were too
close, their hands pawing me, their comments and their
looks getting worse and worse. Noah, unwilling to lose
their business, relaxed the security. So in the guise of
congratulating me, they kept cornering me everywhere
I turned after the show. Even then, I somehow managed.

"Until…he said customers were asking for personal

performances. That they were willing to pay upward of thousands for one dance, that they wanted me to get more familiar with them... Some of the girls told me it wasn't that bad, that they made more money... But all I could see was turning into my mother, hating myself for the rest of my life, falling for one of those men who didn't even know the real me, deluding myself that one of them would actually want me for something more than a quick...

"I couldn't bear to do it. I didn't have the guts to see it through anymore. It just felt as if I would never ever get out of that life if I stayed any longer. There was only so much I was willing to do to repay Andrew's debt."

Men, driven by lust and hunger, leering and pawing at her, because the kind of club that Noah owned wouldn't be anything like the one he had just acquired... The picture her words painted nauseated him. He shot out of the bed, his blood boiling, his emotions raw.

She sat up in the bed, her hair mussed up, her expression so vulnerable that it caught at his chest.

"Dmitri, what is it? Don't, please, look at me like that. As if I..." She didn't finish the words, her throat working conspicuously, her hands fisting the duvet.

But he didn't care what she was feeling. *Theos*, he was drowning in what could have been. "You could have come to me so much sooner. You could have avoided all that. If any of them had gotten his hands on you, if they had forced you into something that you didn't want... *Christos*." He turned and slammed his fist into the wall.

But even the pain that shafted up his knuckles and arm was not enough to release the fear that crawled through his veins.

"Dmitri, you have to understand—"

"Understand what, Jas? You had a choice. My father was an alcoholic bastard but did you know that my mother was a prostitute?" he said bitterly, giving voice to something he had never shared with another soul. "He drank with her money but hated her for it. It ate through him and he took it out on her and me. Half the time, I couldn't stop him because I was such a runt...until I learned to use my speed and my fists...

"She was saving to leave London, just enough so that she could bring me to Giannis in Athens, who was her uncle. She had to hide the money because he took all of it from her. And then just two days before we were set to leave, he found out. He was in one of his drunken rages and he pushed her.

"She hit her head on the wall and died instantly, before I could even catch her. Then he locked the door outside and he ran." He dropped to the bed, his head in his hands, trembling, shivering, still feeling her cold body in his arms. "I sat there for hours, imagining all the different ways I could have saved her. The silence... I have never been able to bear it since. If Andrew hadn't come to look for me as he always did when he heard from the neighbors that my father was in a drunken rage again, I don't know how long I would have been there.

"You know what I thought when Gaspard touched you today, Jas? Fear that I wouldn't be able to save you. And now to hear you so blithely say that's where you have put yourself willingly for so many years..."

He felt as if he was in that moment today. The pain and the fear that ripped through him... He couldn't breathe.

Turning away from her, he put on his discarded trousers, his chest cold as ice. He couldn't bear to look at her, not all that loveliness, that flush to her skin.

Because if he did, he knew either he would be tempted to wring her neck for her recklessness or he would take her against the wall like an animal, her comfort and soreness be damned, just to rid the shiver in his muscles. Just to feel all of her with his rough hands, just to reassure himself that she was here, safe in his arms, beyond that world's reach now…

And then he would never be able to forgive himself.

He needed to leave until he had a better handle on his emotions, until he understood what was happening to him. He found his hands were shaking.

"Dmitri." Her soft entreaty seared through him and he turned.

The sheet wrapped around her nakedness, she rose from the bed like a goddess, and even drowning in fury, he was drawn to her. "Don't, Jas… I can't bear to look at you."

Her arm fell back against her body. The wariness disappeared from her eyes and something else set in. He was almost at the door.

"I hated you for never looking back," she said then, sounding small and broken.

Her words were like a rope that bound him to the room, to her.

"For years, I imagined that you would come back and somehow rescue Andrew and me from that life. I built you up into…this hope in my head when Andrew got worse, when it felt as if I couldn't take another day." He opened his mouth but she raised her hand. "I know the truth now, I do. But when Andrew told me those lies about you giving up on us, all that hope instantly turned to hate. Because, you see, that hatred was easier to bear than the pain.

"I thought you had abandoned me. Just like the rest of them. Like my father, my mum and even Andrew. At his funeral, you were so distant, so out of my sphere, full of pity for me. You stood there so coldly, offering me money, as if that was all I deserved from you. As if I was a problem you wanted to fix and then forget about."

Pity? He had never pitied her. He had looked at her,

eighteen and innocent and full of such blazing hatred for him, and he'd thought she was better off without him...

He hadn't been able to stomach that he had failed at saving another life... That even with all the wealth he had acquired, he had been of no use... The idea of letting Jasmine back in his life, even if he had been able to persuade her in the first place, the fear of failing had been too much...

It was still too much.

"Andrew always said," she continued in that same, small voice, "pride was my biggest shortcoming. The thought of begging you for help, it made me so angry. I wanted you to look at me and not feel pity... I wanted to prove to you that I could somehow make it without your help... Pathetic, right, that even then, I was so fixated on you."

"*Theos*, Jas..."

"Tonight I told myself I had nothing to be ashamed of. That I wasn't going to hold myself responsible for their mistakes, that I... But I'm in your bed and you are looking at me as if you wish you had never laid a finger on me. Exactly what I had always wanted to avoid."

She didn't give him a chance to negate her; she didn't give him a chance to even process everything she had blurted out in that usual blatantly raw way of hers.

Dragging the red sheet behind her, her shoulders a stiff line, she walked away.

Jasmine didn't know how long she stood under the hot spray of the shower after Dmitri had walked out. But there was such cold in her chest that she felt as though she would never warm up ever again.

Dmitri was disgusted by her illustrious career. She had asked him straight and he hadn't denied her. But even worse than his disgust was the turmoil that churned through her gut.

Because even if he had been able to stomach his disgust, she had betrayed herself, hadn't she? She hadn't known what she had been about to say, had only wanted to make him understand why she hadn't come to him for help. Only wanted to make him see that it had been so hard. Only wanted to take away that anguish in his eyes.

Instead, she had blurted out things even she hadn't fully realized, didn't know what to make of.

She rubbed her head, where an ache was beginning. In reality, she was sore all over, between her thighs especially. Her skin felt extrasensitive to the spray of the complicated jets of the shower. On her hips, where his fingers had dug in so hard and held her down when he had been thrusting into her, her scalp where he had held her for his kiss… He was all over her, inside and out.

Fixated on him, really, had she no self-respect left? Was she going to beg him next to keep her in his bed?

He had made love to her—no, sex. It had been explosive sex, yes, but only that, and here she was, pushing her fears, her fixation for him onto his plate. A long jump for a man who had admitted to just wanting her, under extreme conditions, too, to her dumping her sob story over him.

No wonder he had said he couldn't bear to look at her. No wonder he hadn't been able to even stay in the room another minute.

It felt as if there was a lead weight in her chest that she couldn't push down or breathe out, blocking her very breath.

And knowing what she had learned from him today, she wondered if even his attraction to her was a product of his protective nature, couldn't help but wonder if he would ever really see the real her.

Not his friend's sister, that friend whom he thought he hadn't been able to save, not as a way to satisfy the guilt that obviously had settled inside him as a teenager who had seen his mother's horrific death...

But just her, Jasmine Douglas, ex-virgin pole dancer, penniless and with no prospects of a career, weak when it came to helping abusive family members and desperately falling for the teenage boy she had known once.

But hurting all over, she couldn't summon the energy to be angry with herself. She had decided today to carve her own life, to make her own mistakes if that was what it took, to stop living in the shadow of the past.

Maybe her first mistake was to fall for a man who would never see her, much less want her in his life.

She had a career that reminded him of a past he clearly wanted to forget, she had thrown herself at him, first for help and now for sex, and she had blurted out her obsession over him. Why would a man who had everything in the world want a woman like her?

Dmitri stepped out from the house into the open grounds, the desolation and shame he had heard in Jas's voice running through him in an endless loop.

Theos, he had only realized after he had lost it so thoroughly how she had lived with that shame for so long, how low her self-esteem must have been.

He had thought her merely attracted to him, whereas it went so much deeper. And tonight, by telling her about Andrew's deceit, he had torn down the last barrier.

Her words and the weight of them... He was not ready for them. He was never going to be worthy of them.

He saw another shadow join his in the silence and turned.

His suit jacket gone, Stavros stood with his hand on the stone bench. They had spent many nights sitting on the bench, looking at the stars, each increasingly awed by the generosity of the man who had saved them both from certain hell. And determined to their last breath that they would make him proud of them.

Full of integrity and honor, Stavros had taught him so much. But right now, he was the last man Dmitri wanted to see because he wouldn't lie to spare Dmitri's feelings. He wouldn't spare anyone, especially when it came to doing the right thing.

"You seduced her, didn't you?" Stavros finally said, sounding utterly disgusted.

Gritting his jaw tight, Dmitri strove to calm himself. He would not lose it tonight, not again.

"Before you lose it, your little temper tantrum was witnessed by everyone at the party. Then you followed her and neither of you emerged for the rest of the night. Leah was worried about her." The bastard went on, unperturbed. "The interesting thing is that you're pacing here in the middle of the night. Which means at least you feel some regret."

"She was a pole dancer at that club."

The statement fell into the dark silence like a grenade waiting to be detonated. His gaze stunned, Stavros looked as though he was out of words.

"That's not the worst," Dmitri added. He needed to fix the situation, but for the life of him, he still couldn't hate himself for what had happened.

"What is, then?"

"She…she's full of shame over it, still just as stubborn, however, she's very vulnerable to me, some kind of leftover from our past together—" *God only knew why* "—and now I seduced her, yes. So it's a lot worse. If I had known how much she—"

"*Theos*, Dmitri, don't start lying to yourself now."

Dmitri felt it like a lash, loathing Stavros for being right.

He would have taken Jas come what may. That he had even resisted that long was a miracle in itself.

But he could not simply walk away from her. To do so would mean to torture himself eternally about whether she was safe. About who she was with, if there was another man who had taken over his place in her life, whether that man was worthy of her, if he would treat her well...

Christos!

And the thought of Jasmine with any other man but him, the thought of any man taking that smile, that double-edged innocence, of any man kissing her or learning that sensuous body of hers... It drove him crazy.

He had never ever felt this possessive about a woman, only a cold detachment. At most, sympathy when it had come to Anya.

He knew that Jasmine hadn't given herself to him lightly, and telling her that it was a night of madness for him would only hurt her.

And he couldn't do that. He couldn't hurt Jasmine, not when there had been a hundred people in her life who had only ever done that.

The solution, the only solution to the tangle of mess he had created, came to him slowly, quite simple in its brilliance.

His heart seemed to freeze for a moment, and then stuttered into life, pounding even harder after that pause.

"I know what to do," he said softly, the idea settling into his every pore, every cell, sinking into him deep. Tilting the very axis of his life. But he didn't feel in the slightest bit worried. It was perfect for the situation he had created, the right thing finally.

His austere features bathed in shadows, Stavros, if possible, became even tenser. "And what would that be?"

Dmitri sighed, wishing he could walk away without answering his question, without giving a damn. But try as he might, he had never been able to wrench that detachment for Stavros.

Giannis had done a fine job of making them more than brothers. He had made them each other's conscience. "I'll not hurt her, Stavros."

"There's more than one way of hurting, Dmitri. I stole five years of her life, *five years* that I can never return, from Leah. Don't be so blindly arrogant as I was to decide her fate for Jasmine."

"I'm not forcing her into anything, Stavros."

He would not force Jas. He would only give her what would make her happy, do what he should have done all those years ago. He owed Andrew that much, despite Andrew's mistakes; he owed *her* that much. And it wasn't as if he was making a huge sacrifice, either, when all he did was flit from woman to woman, trying to fill the emptiness he felt.

At least, with Jas, there would be the satisfaction of doing the right thing. At least, with Jas, there would be no emptiness. Not when she looked at him like that.

"Dmitri, I'm—"

Dmitri had had enough. He turned away from Stavros and went back to the house. For the first time in forever, he had found something that made him feel as though he was alive again. Something that helped him look in the mirror and see a worthy man.

Something that he was determined to hold on to.

CHAPTER ELEVEN

Two days later, the most beautiful day dawned, as if the elements had decided to behave in the face of such true, abiding love as Jasmine saw in Leah and Stavros's eyes.

A lone tear slid down her cheek as they posed for a picture under the arch of lilies. With her eyes twinkling and her mouth painted a luscious red, Leah was a perfect contrast to Stavros's severely stunning looks.

She was so glad to have witnessed the wedding, the best part in her mind when Dmitri, looking so breathtakingly gorgeous in a black tuxedo, had walked Leah to Stavros and handed her over.

Something had passed between the two men, a sliver of tension that paused the whole tableau, but then Dmitri had kissed Leah's cheek and gone to stand by Stavros.

If she had thought her life strange before, it was nothing compared to the roller coaster of the past two days.

It had been close to dawn when, after hours of tossing and turning, she had fallen into a fitful sleep that night after he had walked out with such anger. While she had refused to cry or pity herself, she had relentlessly wondered where Dmitri had gone. Wondered if he would disappear again.

And then suddenly, he had been there in her bed just as the sun touched everything in the room with a pink glow.

Naked and gloriously, arrogantly masculine, he had been a cocoon of warmth and hardness behind her.

Had she resisted him? Had she even put up a token fight when he had come back to her bed as if he belonged there?

No, all she had felt had been unprecedented joy that he had come back to her, utter relief that he didn't loathe her for what she had told him. She had been weak, yes, but Jasmine didn't know how to be anything else when it came to Dmitri, didn't know how to arrest her heart from jumping into her throat when he looked at her, or how to stop her skin from tingling with one casual touch of his.

At least, the past was all done between them; at least, he still wanted her, she had thought pathetically. When he had given her a breath to think, that was.

Pulling her toward him, he had thrown a muscular, naked leg over her own, his arm a steel band around her waist, his erection already hard and big, nestling against her bottom like it belonged there.

She had moaned and pushed back into him, even as her mind had said she should be doing the opposite. Whispering the wickedest things into her skin, he had sneaked his large hands under her shirt, *his shirt* that she had stolen from his wardrobe at the hotel in London, and found her breasts. Told her he had never been so thoroughly stripped of all good sense, that he had never felt such urgent, devouring need ever before.

There had been such a possessive heat to his words that even now, standing amidst a hundred guests, Jasmine felt the silky slide of those words, as addictive as his knowing touch.

He had stroked her to such a fever pitch that she had forgotten all about how sore she had felt earlier. "Please, Dmitri," she had whispered, apparently the only thing she was capable of saying to him.

Slowly, lazily, he had pushed into her from behind, his teeth digging into her shoulder, his fingers flicking at her

sex with that same lazy rhythm. Rocked them both into
such a slow climax that had nevertheless left her boneless.

As if all his fury had been pushed out of him, as if he
had all the time in the world to enjoy the fire between
them. As if he never wanted to leave her side ever again.

Tears had filled her eyes and she had tried to hide them.
But he had only turned her to him. "No more tears, *glykia
mou*, and no more shame. Whatever you had to do, it's all
over, Jas." He had kissed her temple, then her fluttering
eyelids, her cheeks, and then had held her with such a tight
grip. "Don't judge yourself, don't ever blame yourself for
surviving." He had said it so tenderly that she had buried
her face in his chest and sobbed, years of grief and loneliness pushing out of her in waves.

And he had soothed her, and hugged her, and fallen
asleep next to her.

When she had woken up again, it had been past noon.
A single, long-stemmed red rose had been by the pillow
along with a note and a velvet case.

Her heart had slammed against her rib cage when she
had run a reverent finger against the soft velvet. Sitting
up, she had reached for the note first.

"Will be back the afternoon of the wedding day. Have
to get something ready. Wear this for me."

Her breath had stuttered out of her at the sight of the
delicately wired diamond necklace, along with matching earrings and bracelet. It had looked utterly expensive
and somehow he had arranged for it to be delivered in a
matter of hours. She had seen a necklace like that once
in London at Tiffany & Co. and had blanched from even
asking the price.

Something about accepting it right after what they had
done hadn't sat well with her. She was already indebted
to him, they had the strangest relationship going on and

the last thing Jas wanted was to lose the little pride she had left.

And that he had left her that little note meant more to her than anything that he could have gifted her.

She fingered the diamond pendant that she had worn instead, hoping he would understand.

Every inch of her thrummed as she waited for the ceremony to be over so that she could tell him all her news. More than anything, she couldn't wait to just hold him again.

The crowd of guests erupted into laughter then, and she turned to see Stavros pick up Leah in his arms and head for the house. She found herself smiling again.

Corded arms wrapped around her from behind. She let out a breathless little gasp as his powerful thighs straddled her, his arousal evoking that powerfully intoxicating need freely in her veins.

She felt the press of his soft lips against her neck and trembled. Long fingers instantly laced with hers, anchoring her. He felt so good and warm around her that her heart took a little tumble in her chest.

"You smell divine, *moro mou*. I can't wait to taste you all over again."

She half turned, trying to speak with a dry mouth. "Dmitri, I have something—"

"You wanted to dance the other night, didn't you?"

Without waiting for her answer, not that she would have refused, he tugged her to the dance floor that had been erected to the side. The grounds looked like they were straight out of a fairy tale as little Moroccan lanterns illuminated the path and cast beautiful shadows everywhere. A sweet smell wafted over from the orange groves.

Dusk wasn't far away and the party was in full swing. A little signal from Dmitri and the band instantly shifted to a slow tune instead of the peppy Greek number. In such a short time, the world suddenly seemed like a wonderful place, and she didn't doubt that it was because of the man who seemed to entrench himself more and more in her heart.

His hands went around her and Jasmine found herself looking straight into his eyes.

Dancing with Dmitri was like eating the most deliciously decadent chocolate, except the sensations were everywhere instead of just in her mouth. His movements effortlessly elegant; he maneuvered them around the floor with a fluid grace that was far from the boy who had used his fists for survival.

Feeling light-headed even though she hadn't touched a drop of alcohol, she put her cheek on his shoulder and looked around.

Leah's wedding list was a who's-who of the fashion world, ranging from models to designers to fashion magazine editors. Wherever she looked on the dance floor and elsewhere, there were stunning beauties, each one more gorgeous and sophisticated than the next. But it was the list of their accomplishments that stung.

What is he doing with me? an insidious voice whispered in her mind, and she tried to tune it out.

She could feel more than one woman's gaze slide to Dmitri surreptitiously, had seen more than one woman come on to him in the guise of polite chitchat.

Because if there was one thing she knew, it was that kind of lust, the one that only wanted the package without knowing what was beneath.

All they saw was a spectacularly gorgeous man with wealth, power and raw sexuality. *I know him like none of you ever will*, she thought with a fierceness she had never known before.

Her hands tightened over his shoulders before she even

realized. *Mine*, she wanted to say in an utterly possessive way.

One muscled thigh grazing hers, Dmitri tipped her chin
up. "You're tense. Is something wrong?"

"No," she replied, determined to not let her stupid inse-
curities ruin what was the most wonderful evening of her
life. She would make something of herself, she promised
herself. She would make him proud of her even if it took
her the rest of her life.

Bolstered by it, she leaned her head on his shoulder and
let his body guide her into the soft rhythm.

For a few moments, they said nothing, sinking into the
sensuous silence that was filled with languorous promises. Every move reminded her of how he had moved inside her, every glance he sent her way a promise of the
night to come.

"You dance like a dream," she whispered.

Their relationship had begun in a strange place, a bed
of all places, and even after two days, she couldn't seem
to look at him and not remember the erotic intimacy of
what they had done.

If she looked at his mouth, her lower belly clenched as
if it remembered the havoc he had wreaked on it. If she
looked at his hands, her hips remembered how he had held
her down for him.

"Giannis, if you can believe it, made us take classes.
He was determined to transform Stavros and me from
the little thugs we were." She shivered as he pulled her
closer. "But I'm not at all surprised that you move like
every man's fantasy."

Her gaze flew to his, but it was only full of a wicked
light. There was no judgment in his tone, implied or otherwise. It was her own shame that ricocheted through her,
that led her to drop her gaze.

He tipped her chin up. "You dance beautifully, Jas,"

he said so tenderly that she couldn't help but smile in return, warmed to the farthest corners of her heart by the depth of his perception.

Stepping back, he looked at her from her hair in an elegant knot to the pendant and the elegant knee-length beige silk dress that Leah had chosen for her, all the way to her feet tucked in nude-colored pumps.

Tingling at his leisurely perusal, she reached for his hand when he frowned.

"You're not wearing the diamond necklace. Why?"

He had spoken softly, yet the displeasure in his tone was clear. "I…"

"Let's get out of here."

He didn't wait for her answer. Clasping her fingers, he tugged her off the dance floor and through the throng of guests, to a path that went away from the crowd.

After another couple of minutes, they arrived at a side door to the house, and then they were in a study that was utterly masculine from the dark brown leather sofas to a huge mahogany table to the scent of cigars that permeated it.

When voices filtered through an open window, Dmitri closed it with a firm click.

"Now." Turning to her, he lifted her over the table, pushed her legs apart as far as the dress allowed, which was indecent enough for her, and stood between them until she was straddling him. "All I have been able to think about is this…"

He claimed her mouth with a hunger that buckled her knees. Instantly, Jasmine was lost in a sea of spiraling sensations.

With a hand on his chest, she pushed at him, and his mouth released hers and slid lower to her neck.

"Please, Dmitri, wait. I want to talk."

"I'm not used to being denied what I want, *pethi mou*,"

he breathed against the pulse in her neck, while his thigh lodged square against her aching sex. "And I want you, need you more than I need air."

With that, he moved his leg and tremors spread through her lower belly. Her hands on his shoulders, Jasmine moved, needing that pressure to push her to the edge.

An arrogant, utterly masculine smile on his face, he obliged. And the satisfaction in that male gaze told Jasmine how easily and effortlessly she was playing into his arms. If she didn't hold her own even a little now, she never would be able to in the future, she realized. However murky the future was right now.

She dug her teeth into his lower lip and pulled, until he looked up with a guttural groan. "I want to talk, so hands off, Dmitri."

He ran a long finger over his lower lip, his eyes threatening retribution. Jasmine held her breath, knowing that she wouldn't last a minute if he didn't back off.

"Please." She pouted, lowering her voice. "If you let me talk first, then I'll do whatever you want tonight."

He turned his neck this way and that, and his broad chest rose and fell. It was like watching a predator take a step back from his prey. "So talk. And tell me why you're not wearing the diamond set I ordered for you?"

In the face of his ruthlessly direct question, she floundered. God, had she ever thought this man frivolous and uncaring? The intensity of his looks, his touch, even his questions spun her head. She lifted the diamond with not-so-steady fingers. "You already gave me a diamond."

"That's all I could afford then. Now I can—"

"It was far too expensive." She injected some steel into her words, and when he scowled, she added hurriedly, "Really, where am I going to wear it to, Dmitri? I have no need for such—"

"You'll have lots of occasions." Masculine satisfaction

dripped from every word. "Tomorrow morning, there will be a stylist here. Order yourself a new wardrobe, everything you want."

"You're just angry that I steal your shirts, aren't you?" she quipped, trying to hide her anxiety.

He kissed her then, just a quick touch of their mouths. "I don't think I've ever seen anything sexier than you wearing my shirt, *matia mou*. But I—"

"I have some really exciting news," she said, interrupting what she sensed was another argument she wouldn't win right now. A thread of unease began to permeate her mood, like the charge that built in the air long before the storm burst.

"What is it?"

"You remember Gaspard." She covered his mouth when his frown turned into a scowl. "Anyway, he referred me to a modeling agency. The head of the agency, this superstylish, sophisticated woman, she was here this afternoon. She said Gaspard had excellent taste when it came to faces, asked Leah about me, and Leah introduced us. Dmitri, she wants me to come in for a screen test in Athens as soon as I can manage it.

"It's true I'm older than the models they sign on but she said I had a different kind of face, whatever that means. Isn't that just great?" Her tone trailed off at the end there as Dmitri's expression remained the same. "Dmitri?"

"It sounds great, *pethi mou*," he said finally, his brow clearing, "but a career in modeling, this is what you want?" His accent suddenly became more pronounced than she had ever heard it.

Her shoulders slumping, Jasmine struggled to keep her voice upbeat. "I've no idea what I want, but it's not as if I have a degree or experience in a worthwhile field, is it? And I'm broke. I thought, why not give this a chance? Eventually, I have to start making a living again and then there's that gazillion pounds that I owe you." The last bit she had added with a smile, because her skin cooled as if there was a chill in the room.

The look in Dmitri's eyes was near lethal. "That debt means nothing between us after what happened two nights ago. As for making a living, I'll take care of you, Jasmine."

She tilted her chin. "And I told you that I won't be your mistress. You can't just come to me at midnight and send me gifts in the morning. That's not what I want, *now or ever.*"

"No, I don't like that option, either."

As if he were a magician, he pulled out a small box from somewhere. Her heart slammed so hard that Jasmine gasped. A diamond ring, a princess cut with tiny ones set around it, glittered and winked at her. His gaze remained shadowed as he looked at her. "Marry me, *thee mou,* and we'll never talk of debts and mistresses ever again."

Every inch of her froze as he slid the ring onto her boneless finger and the damning, breath-stealing, soul-wrenching thing was that the ring fit her so perfectly. The cold weight of it felt unfamiliar against her skin, her breath ballooning up in her lungs.

Jasmine looked at the ring for several seconds. Shock and joy roped together in her veins, and beneath all of it, fear pulsed.

She looked up and tried to smile, but it wouldn't come. Her hands on his chest, she expelled a long breath. "I don't know what to say, Dmitri. Wow, I just… This is… I…"

Clasping her cheeks, he took her mouth in a long kiss that stole all the air from her lungs again. "Say yes, Jas." His hands moved to her back and pulled her closer to him, until all she knew was Dmitri and his broad shoulders, and his corded strength and his thrilling words. She felt as if she was floating on a different plane, far removed from reality.

"I have the license ready and we can marry here tomorrow evening. Once we tell them, Leah and Stavros will stay on. Leah undoubtedly will have a dress that's as gorgeous as you are in her wedding collection, and everything else has already been taken care of."

Burying her face in his chest, Jasmine willed her racing pulse to slow down, to give her a chance to breathe. And the moment her heart settled to normal, something else followed. "Tomorrow?" Only the one word escaped her.

Stroking her lip with his tongue, he breathed his answer into her mouth. "Yes. I want us to marry as soon as possible. That way…you don't have to worry about making a living, don't have to jump into something that you're not sure about.

"Take a couple of courses at the university if you like. Just take it easy, *matia mou*. Or if you decide all you want to be is Mrs. Karegas, that's perfectly fine, too."

Her head spinning, Jasmine pushed away from him and slid off the desk. "You don't want me to work?"

He shrugged, his hands in his trouser pockets. "I don't ever want you to worry, Jas, about anything. Everything I have is yours."

"Wow, Dmitri. I…I'm drowning here," she said, feeling dizzy with the number of emotions claiming her.

"All you have to say is yes, Jas. And tomorrow night, we can set off on our honeymoon to wherever you want to go."

Impulsively, she hugged him, the scent of him pushing the word *yes* to her lips.

And yet something held her back; something punctured the utter joy of the moment. Panic fueling her movements, she jerked away. "Wait, Dmitri, let me breathe, won't you?"

He smiled and nodded, his gaze moving hungrily over her.

Rings and diamond sets, dresses and wardrobes, it

seemed there was nothing Dmitri couldn't wait to lavish upon her. But love... There was nothing of love in his words. That was it.

Because she loved him with all her heart, she thought in a daze. Somewhere between knifing him and kissing him, she had irrevocably fallen in love with him, had moved from a childhood obsession to feeling as though she would never have enough of him.

It had been that moment when he had told her about Andrew's deception. Or maybe the moment when he had called her perfection. Or when he had held her so tenderly as she had sobbed her heart out.

Everything in her life was shifting and uncertain, but how she felt about Dmitri... There was no doubt about that.

Shaking at the realization, utterly terrified now, she looked at him.

He had removed his jacket, and the white shirt hugged the breadth of his shoulders, a perfect contrast to the olive skin. He looked so utterly gorgeous and he wanted to marry her.

He could have any woman in the world. Why did he want her?

Did he love her?

Did he know how she felt about him? She had never really tried to hide her feelings from him, had she?

Questions burned through her head in an endless loop, slowly but surely siphoning off the warmth from her.

But suddenly now she wanted to hide away from him, wished she could give herself time to let the truth sink in.

Why else would he want to marry you? the hopeful part of her, the part that had forever loved everything about him, said.

Her thoughts still scrambled, she turned to him and said the first thing she could think of. "You'll give up your playboy status? You'll give up all those women? Because marriage is nothing without fidelity and respect, Dmitri."

He didn't seem in the least bit offended by her questions. On the contrary, a smile cut grooves in his cheek as though he wanted nothing but to allay her fears. "I will be the most faithful husband in the world, *pethi mou*. I'll give even Stavros a run for it, yes?"

Reaching her, he put his hands on her hips, kissed her temple. And standing in his arms, soaking in his words, Jasmine desperately wanted to say yes.

"I'll do everything in my power to make you happy, Jas, to take care of you. You'll want for nothing, you'll see."

Just like that, Jas felt her answer float away from her lips. Her happiness, her well-being, all Dmitri talked about was her. As though she was one of his possessions—a well-oiled bike, a smoothly run nightclub, a well-maintained portfolio that only kept on giving.

What about him?

What did he feel for her?

What had shifted that he wanted to marry her?

Still grappling with how deep her feelings ran, how much weight each word of his carried with her, Jas felt his words like a rope binding her to him. "What about love, Dmitri?" she said finally. Her chest was so tight, her fingers chillingly cold as if she had dunked them in ice.

He became absolutely still, but something uncoiled in those gray eyes. "What about love, Jas?"

So he was going to torture this out of her. "Do you love me, Dmitri?"

"No, but then I don't believe I'm capable of it, Jas. I feel a certain affection for Leah, loyalty for Stavros, but that's about the breadth of my emotional range. And you—" her breath hung in her throat "—you'll have my fidelity and my friendship."

Her hopes fell away, his words shattering her heart into

a thousand pieces inside her chest. She slumped against the table, her limbs shaking uncontrollably.

He reached her instantly and caught her. "*Theos*, Jas, I thought you would be happy. I thought this was what you wanted."

And there it was…the final proof in his own words.

Cradled against him, Jas felt herself tearing into two halves, one gleefully, treacherously ecstatic that this strong, powerful, honorable man would be hers, and the other, warning away from a fate that could leech away every ounce of joy from her life.

If she married him because he made her feel safe and because he was offering friendship and because of the wild heat between them, if she willingly went into this knowing that he would never even open himself to the possibility of love, knowing that his vows were born out of guilt and a protective instinct that was a mile wide while she, bound to him irrevocably, would wait for him to open his heart, while she crucified herself wondering if it was something within herself…

The fear that she had been holding at bay for so many days, *years actually*, twisted and swelled inside her…until she saw herself turning into her worst nightmare. Her mother had waited and wasted away her entire life for a man who had never looked back.

Would that be her fate, too, if she weakened in this minute? Was her choice to smash her heart into pieces now or wait for it to fall apart piece by piece over years?

"I never wanted you to marry me, Dmitri. I would have settled for…" Her words seemed to dissolve on her lips when he pinned her with his gaze.

Because then, she could hope for a better future than the one he had so thoroughly mapped out for her. Because then, she had foolishly thought, she would make herself worthy of him, that she would somehow make him proud of her.

A stillness seemed to creep up into his face while his gaze, that gaze that had never been able to lie to her, burned with a ferocity that he had kept leashed until now. "I offered marriage because you deserve better, Jas."

Her throat was so thick with ache that she thought she might be sick.

God, if he talked about her one more time as if she were something to be cosseted and protected, she was going to scream. And then crumple into a heap. "Have you offered marriage to every woman you have ever slept with? Or is it a special offer reserved for virgins?"

"*Theos*, you're different from the numerous other women I screwed. There, is that enough?"

"How? How am I different?"

"You're Andrew's sister." Jas wanted to cover her ears and scream. "And you're the most annoyingly stubborn woman I've ever met."

Before she knew, he was clasping her to him and plundering her mouth with his.

It was a kiss meant to possess, to captivate, to lay claim. And still, Jas lost herself to it. Lost herself in the erotic strokes of his wicked tongue, lost herself in the heat he so easily stroked into life, lost herself in the hard body.

Lost herself in the man who promised her so much except the one thing she really needed.

One hand cupped her breast reverently while the other pulled her snug against him to feel his rigid shaft. Her breath left her in a soft flutter, tears she couldn't fight anymore spilling onto her cheeks.

"I promise you, Jas, I have never known anything like this fire between us... You would walk away from this?"

She caressed his jaw with her mouth, breathing in the scent of him. "I have to."

How could something that felt so good eventually turn out to be bad for her? Her body, pulsing with need, seemed to find it impossible to grasp.

Steeling her spine, she pushed away from him for the last time. "I can't marry you, Dmitri. I have barely found myself after years of living buried under others' mistakes, others' addictions. I can't do that to myself again." *Not even for you.*

"I'm promising you a life that will lack for nothing. How is it not—"

"But this is about guilt, *your guilt.* I'm your project for all the things you failed at. For not being able to save your mother all those years ago, for your supposed failure with Andrew, for not *saving* me from my tasteless past soon enough.

"All of this—" her voice broke, a deluge of tears knocking at her eyes "—is only because you want to feel better about yourself."

"I know how you feel about me." His control slipped then, his anger spewing into his words. As if she was the one hurting him, as if somehow this was all her fault. As if she had somehow damaged him. "I know what that night meant to you. How does it matter when I'm offering everything I can of myself?"

Was this how it felt when one's heart broke? Did the world keep on turning? "It's because I feel so much that I can't accept this. I can't let my love for you break me, Dmitri.

"Because I do love you. I love you so much that there's this voice inside that's *screaming* that I'm stupid to walk away from this, that I should grab it with both hands. That I should take what little I can get of you." She grabbed her head, as if she could silence it. "And it won't stop. I don't think it will ever stop."

"Then, listen to it. For once, *thee mou*, do what is good for you. Don't walk away, Jas."

Grasping the door handle, Jas looked at him. The thing that hurt the most was that he didn't understand. He didn't see how painful it was for her to walk away, how hard it would be for her to accept the little he gave of himself when she wanted everything.

When he walked toward her, she shook her head. "No. Don't touch me and don't come to my room. Don't…do anything more for me, Dmitri, please."

CHAPTER TWELVE

DMITRI DIDN'T KNOW how he had made it through the night.

He remembered pacing the study like a caged animal. It was how he had felt in that first year when Giannis had brought him to this very house. He had once called it house-training a wild animal.

He had, through will hanging by a thread, kept himself in the study. Every cell in him wanted to convince her the only way he knew but then he told himself she deserved better.

So he paced and drank and paced some more, trying to think of ways to stop her. It was now morning and he was no closer to a solution.

Except the renewed resolve to keep her in his life. And the panic that flared at the thought that he might fail, that he had somehow lost Jas irrevocably, and that it was nothing compared to all the losses he had lived through...

For a man who had floated through most of his adult life loathing his inability to feel anything, loathing the fact that his father had stolen more than his mother from him, it was like drowning after being parched for years.

He needed dark, blistering coffee to ground himself, to make sure he didn't do anything that he would regret later. His shirt half undone, his hair in disarray, he reached the breakfast room.

The scent of sweet pastries and coffee filled the room, the house blissfully silent after last night.

Dressed in a long-sleeved sweater and slacks, his hair still wet from the shower, Stavros looked like the very picture of matrimonial bliss. Their gazes met and held.

Stavros poured some of the thick, dark coffee and pushed a cup toward Dmitri. "You look terrible."

"Why aren't you in bed with your wife, Stavros? Or better yet, why aren't you gone yet? This is my estate now."

A brow raised, Stavros stared at him. "I was waiting for you."

Dmitri took a long sip and felt marginally human again. He ran a hand over his jaw and felt the bristle. *Theos*, he must look like the savage he felt like. He would have to shower and shave before he went up to see her. He still didn't know what he was going to say.

Do you love me, Dmitri?

He had offered her everything and she had asked for the one thing he didn't know how to do.

Fear and confusion like he had never known before gripped his insides.

It felt as though overnight he had lost something, something precious he hadn't even known he had. Not for a moment had he thought she would say no.

If she loved him, wouldn't she want to spend her life with him?

He finished his coffee and turned toward the door. To hell with civilizing himself.

She was the one person in the world who knew what he was beneath the mask he showed the world. She hadn't even relented until he had showed himself to her. Had goaded him, challenged him...had made him feel so much again.

There was no way he was just letting her walk away from this.

He had almost reached the door when Stavros spoke. "She's not here, Dmitri."

The words hit Dmitri as if they were fists he couldn't evade. His breath knocked out of him. He didn't think, even for an infinitesimal second, that Stavros might be talking about Leah; he couldn't delude himself even for a second that his entire world hadn't just cracked under his very feet.

And fury came to his aid, filling the hollowness in his gut. "What do you mean she left?"

"Leah said Jasmine was waiting for her when she came down. That she begged her to help her leave. That she couldn't stay another minute here. So I had the jet readied and she left."

His gut dropped. "You let her go back to that pit that she calls home?"

"Jasmine said she never wanted to go back there, asked Leah if she had a job for her, even carrying coffee back and forth at her factory. Since she has the screen test in two days, Leah insisted that she stay at her old flat in Athens for a little while. She went with her because Jasmine looked as if she was barely keeping it together."

Dmitri exhaled a relieved breath, once again eternally glad that Leah and Stavros had such generous hearts.

And the relief was followed by a cavern of longing ripping open in his gut.

He slid into the chair and buried his head in his hands. He should be glad she was gone, shouldn't he? If she was safe, why didn't the weight on his chest lift?

When had wanting to keep her safe changed to missing her as if he had lost a vital part of himself?

If this was what it felt like to lose Jasmine after a mere matter of weeks, what would it feel like after a month, a year or a decade of the marriage he had proposed? What would it feel like to lose her forever, to become the man who had pushed her into losing herself?

And suddenly, he understood her panic. He understood how hard he had made it for her, how strong she was to have walked away.

He realized the truth in her words. It had not been about protecting her at all, just as she had said.

It had all been about him. About pacifying his guilt, about his selfish needs, about keeping her in his life, about taking everything she gave without reserve but giving nothing of himself.

Was that what he had always done? Had the gut-wrenching pain of his mother's death made him a self-fulfilling prophecy, a man who only chose the shallowest of relationships, the most ephemeral of things to fill his life?

Could he reach for more now? Could he risk that pain, knowing that he might have lost his chance with Jasmine? Wouldn't that pain still be better than this emptiness?

He felt Stavros's arm on his shoulder, feeling as though nothing would ever touch him again. "I thought you would be angry with me for interfering," Stavros said softly, as if he knew how raw Dmitri felt inside. "I thought you would come at me with your fists."

But then, nothing in the world had ever laid him this low.

Breathing through a throat rough with emotion, Dmitri shook his head. "Because you did what I was unable to do and cared enough about what she wants? I was determined to not let the past matter, Stavros. I was determined that it wouldn't leave a mark on me. And yet…"

"It is a part of you, Dmitri."

"I hurt her and I don't know how to fix it now. I don't know how to tell her that I need her in my life, and not for all the reasons I made her believe.

"*Theos*, everything we have built, everything I told myself I needed to fill my life, they mean nothing to me if she's not there."

Stavros squeezed his shoulder and left without another word. As if he understood, for once, that there was nothing he could do to help Dmitri.

Long after noon gave way to dusk, Dmitri sat there in that vast kitchen in that house that Giannis had given to him, where he had learned to be civilized, where he had learned that he didn't have to live with pain, where he had learned that not all men were alcoholic, out-of-control cowards like his father. Where he had learned that he could be more than the product of his genes and his father's abuse.

But more than anything else, Giannis had tried so hard to give Dmitri back his self-worth. Suddenly, Dmitri was filled with purpose, hope and a yearning.

If he had to spend the rest of his life waiting for Jasmine, proving to Jasmine that he needed her in his life, that he absolutely couldn't breathe for knowing that she was somewhere in the world and not his...

He would do it. He would show her his heart; he would show her that his life was empty without her.

Fashion photographers, Jasmine discovered to her utter shock over the next few weeks, were apparently a whole other species who thought they didn't have to follow the dictates of polite society.

One week into her new career and she felt as though she had been steamrolled, turned inside out for everyone to see.

Maybe it was that she had gotten used to seeing the very obvious appreciation and lust in her customers' eyes when she had taken the stage at the nightclub, even though she'd hated it at that time. Or maybe because, apparently, she was the twenty-three-year-old village idiot, who knew nothing about how the fashion industry worked, amidst models, both men and women, younger and more experienced than her.

That first week after she had left Dmitri—because her whole life was now clearly demarcated by that one event, before Dmitri and after Dmitri, as if nothing else could even come close to holding significance in her life—had been a seamless blur of outward activity, more than she had seen in the past five years of her life, and a growing sense of stillness within.

She found herself asking the same question during the strangest moments during the day.

Had she thrown away her only chance at life with the man she adored in the name of weakness? Had she traded the happiness of at least a few days for the emptiness in her gut?

The agency had loved her after the screen test, calling her their next big find. With help from Stavros's lawyer, without whom she would have signed away her entire life, she signed a very tight, time-limited exclusive contract with the agency.

Sick of moping around the flat while she waited, she had made a habit of visiting Leah every day at her factory after a rigorous workout at the gym next door to keep in shape, and really, to keep the ever-gnawing void in her stomach at bay.

There wasn't a minute that she didn't think about Dmitri, a day where she felt like she would ever be normal again.

It had been a month of torture, as she started calling it.

Because while she had been crying herself to sleep every night, Dmitri, it seemed, was taking the media and the world by storm.

It had begun when she had heard that the huge char-

ity event organized by Anya Ivanova, the model he had
helped, had sported his custom-designed Bugatti bike.

The next week had been an expose about his yacht,
which apparently was currently being bought by a Russian oil billionaire. And the most shocking thing of all
was when a courier had arrived at her doorstep one evening, following a call from Dmitri's executive assistant,
to pick up the diamond set he had gifted her and she had
never worn.

Then came another lengthy phone call with his lawyer
about setting up steps for her to pay off her debt to him.
Something she had insisted on.

What was he doing? she wondered, going half-mad.
Was he moving? Desperate to understand what he was
up to, she spent countless hours trawling luxury real estate websites to see if he had put Giannis's beautiful estate also up for sale.

But not once had she heard anything from him, even
indirectly through Leah, whom she saw regularly.

Had he decided that he had had an easy escape?

Then came her first client, a lifesaver in so many ways.

In the first week of the photo shoot as the new face of a
small Italian shoe company, she had learned what a stress-
ful, hardworking slog it was. Especially if it was something you fell into as an escape from throwing yourself
at the man who didn't love you.

Her first shoot with the photographer, apparently a
Spanish genius called Eduardo de Cervantes, had been
the worst. Eduardo possessed no polish like Gaspard had,
whatever monster he was in his personal life, kept losing
his temper when she couldn't get a pose or expression
right, and at the end of the longest three hours of her life,
had called the whole shoot utterly useless and walked
away, spewing curses in Spanish.

If she had been the type to burst into tears, that moment had been it. But somehow, or maybe because her heart felt as if it was already encased in ice, she had made it through it without turning into a puddle.

They had finally had a breakthrough on the third day when he had once again snarled at her about not having a sensuous bone in her body and she, smarting about the one thing she was good at, had grabbed his hand, marched him over to the next floor where she had heard they had been shooting a firemen-themed calendar, had then proceeded to show her particular talent with a pole.

It had been quite the glorious thing to see Eduardo's jaw hit his chest. And the transformation in his demeanor and her response to it had been thrilling. Suddenly, it was as if he knew what to say to her, how to tease her into a pose, how to make her pout, and she'd eased into the rapport they'd suddenly had going, put her trust in him.

She wasn't exactly an overnight sensation but still her success had given her a new kind of confidence.

After those first two weeks, November passed in a haze as her initial contract with the shoe company got extended to cover Europe and North American markets, and then a fashion magazine invited her to do their Christmas runway show.

She didn't miss the irony of the fact that, once again, it was her genes that had enabled her entry into the fashion world. Not that it was without hard work.

The money began to flow in. Not huge chunks, not enough to cover her humongous debt to Dmitri, but enough to give her a new insight into life, enough to make her appreciate life and all the exciting opportunities it held. Enough to tell her that her heart wasn't in modeling and that it was only a way to give herself a cushion, and that she didn't want to live this life he had given her back doing something she didn't absolutely, gloriously enjoy.

Which in turn brought her back to Dmitri and how much she enjoyed doing anything with him.

Somehow she had thought she would feel better once she was self-sufficient. Maybe even hoped that the magic of being in love with him would dim with distance and independence.

If so, she was apparently as foolish as Andrew.

Some days, all she could manage was to come home to the flat, wash her makeup and the day's shoot off herself, drink her smoothie and fall into bed. As if waiting to strike her at a weak moment, the grief and pain came then.

She thought of laughing, smiling Andrew who had loved her so much and yet given in to his weakness, of how she had made excuses for him because she had thought he had never had a break. She thought of her mother, who had had two loving, affectionate children, and yet had chosen to lose herself in drink.

But Dmitri, who had suffered so much worse, had not only made it, but had also looked out for them. It didn't matter that he'd had help in the form of Giannis and Stavros. It was he who had made something of himself, made himself more than the product of his father's abuse and violence.

So why couldn't she?

But you have already, an arrogant voice sounding quite like Dmitri said.

And it was as if the entire world remained the same chaotic, sometimes utterly soul-crushing, sometimes gorgeously life-giving mystery that it was, but it was how she looked at it, how she looked at herself that underwent a seismic shift.

Even through the darkest, coldest, most depressing night of her life in the past decade, she had never once accepted defeat, had never once surrendered herself to things beyond her control; she had never once let herself drown.

It would have been so easy to give in. She had had all the temptation. And with Dmitri, *God*, she'd had more than temptation.

But she had walked away. It had torn her in two but she had walked away, hadn't she? And she had kept on walking.

She had stared her weakness in the eye and not only emerged from it unscathed, but she had made something out of herself. She had stood without flinching in the face of a cruel, unfamiliar world that seemed to be even more mercurial than her mother's moods and stayed the course.

Despite the results to the contrary, why did she keep measuring herself by Andrew's and her mother's sins?

She was not them. She was Jasmine Douglas, former pole dancer, maybe model and something fiercer in the future.

She was stronger and she deserved any happiness she could get. And her happiness, oh, her very heart was with Dmitri. It would always be.

Everything changed as if floodgates had been opened.

She didn't care that he wanted her because he thought she needed protection, that he did it out of guilt.

So what if he wasn't willing to call it love? So what if he thought he was incapable of it?

He had protected her, cared for her, helped her emerge from her own shame; he had counted her worthy even before she had counted herself. If that wasn't love... Every second she was with Dmitri, she lived and loved more than she had the rest of her life.

She had never given up before, even when the odds had been stacked high against her. Not on her brother, not on her mother, and now, she wouldn't give up on the most important thing in her life—she wouldn't give up on Dmitri.

She would prove to him how much he already loved her, even if it took her the rest of her life.

CHAPTER THIRTEEN

ONCE SHE HAD made up her mind, Jasmine couldn't bear to wait another minute before she went to see Dmitri. Even worse was the fact that he was in the same city yet so far away from her.

It took her another week to finish her current photo shoot and find a free day, so close to Christmas. Another day then to drum up enough guts to ask Stavros, when she saw him, about Dmitri's whereabouts.

He was in London, Stavros had said pithily. When she had probed as to why, he had muttered, "Personal business." Jasmine had a feeling Stavros hadn't wanted to give out any information at all.

When she had asked him, tethering her desperation just by the skin of her teeth, when he would return, he had said today. When Leah had glared at him, he had added that he would return to his Athens flat because they had a superimportant deal he was finalizing to talk about.

Jasmine had barely held her curiosity in check, because she wanted to know what deal was so important two days before Christmas and what Dmitri's personal business was, because it was sure as hell not about her, and not with Leah or Stavros because they had both been in Athens the past week.

Acknowledging that nothing was going to make what she had to do easier, she showered that afternoon and dressed in black pencil jeans and a royal blue sleeveless silk shirt that highlighted her physique without hugging. She paired the blouse with a sleekly cut white jacket. Black pumps and her hair in a French braid and she was ready to go.

Wouldn't you have a better chance if you were dressed to attract his attention? a devilish voice inside whispered, but she shushed it.

She wanted them to talk rationally. She wanted to tell him everything she had thought of, and dressing demurely would help.

Dmitri's flat turned out to be a penthouse on a pedestrian street in the city center of Athens, only a short walk from an art gallery and a lively café where she had spent more than a few hours gathering courage and drinking far too much of the dark, thick Greek coffee.

Wired and anxious was not a good combination, her stomach decided, going on a downward dive while the lift took her to the seventh floor.

A landscaped atrium was across the entrance, revealing breathtaking views of the Acropolis and Lycabettus Hill on either side. Early-afternoon sunlight amplified the open plan.

Jasmine stood awestruck, taking in the warm appeal of the soaring ceilings and the refined wood finish. She walked through the atrium and noted that the penthouse expanded on either side, and ahead was a large heated pool overlooking the spectacular Athens skyline.

Hadn't Leah mentioned to her that Dmitri's flat was all chrome and steel and utterly soulless?

A small sitting area was by the side of the pool. Her heart hammering against her rib cage now that she was here, Jasmine stood by the pool, not wanting to check each room, and there seemed to be a lot, for him.

She was wondering if she should have called him first when she heard footsteps behind her. Each and every one of her senses tingled as if someone had sent a spark through her body.

Bracing herself, Jasmine turned.

Black sweatpants hanging low on his hips, his torso naked, there was Dmitri, standing only a foot away from her. Jet-black hair cut to enhance that narrow, angular face, olive skin gleaming like the finest velvet while beads of sweat clung to the ridges of muscle, he looked like he had done after he had made love to her that next morning.

He leaned against the wall, as if he was not at all surprised that she was here.

Jas fought to control her instantly volatile reaction—tingling skin, racing pulse, the sudden and insistent tug in her lower belly—and failed. Heat flashed over her as she realized he had blocked her path purposely. Behind her was the narrow stretch of pool and then the skyline of Athens, and before her Dmitri, looking at her as if he couldn't wait to devour her.

That brought on images of his dark head between her legs and the way he had devoured her, and she pressed her legs instinctively together, the denim rasping against her inner thighs, and then their eyes met and she knew he was remembering it, too, because there was such an intense hunger in his gaze…

Her breath rushed out of her in a shuddering exhale.

She might as well have walked in in her underwear for all the time she had spent carefully choosing her outfit.

"That would have been nice after the torture of the past few weeks," he said, pushing off the wall, and Jasmine realized she had said it out loud.

It was as if she was standing in a bubble of sensual haze and didn't have her usual faculties.

She wet her lips, searching for how to start what she wanted to say. "You've been busy the past few weeks," she finally managed to say.

"As have you, *pethi mou*" came the soft drawl.

"What's going on, Dmitri? Why so many changes?"

"I decided that I needed to remove all the empty, meaningless things I have filled my life with. All the things that I believed made it better. All the things that I used to hide from the truth." He ran his knuckles over her cheek as if he couldn't help himself.

"When Stavros told me you had asked about me..." He swallowed and looked away for a second. When he spoke again, his voice was almost steady. "Tell me, Jas, what are you doing here?"

"I'm traveling to New York for a shoot in January. And I didn't want to leave without... I came by to tell you that I want a compromise between us."

He was closer and the masculine scent of him drenched her pores. She inhaled a long breath as if she were a junkie getting her fix.

He was her drug, she realized. But unlike her mother's and brother's choice of poison, he made her stronger, bolder, more *her* than anything she had ever been.

His gaze lingered over her mouth. "What sort of compromise?"

Oh, how tempted she was to taste that mouth of his again... "I want to be with you. I want us to give our relationship a try. But you can't ask me to marry you again. Not like that. At least, not until we decide together that it is a step we want to take, until we decide it is what we want."

He flinched. She knew he did because she was standing so close, breathing in every nuance in his face. Slowly, he took a step back and studied her. "But you want this?"

Her heart racing again, she nodded. There was a bittersweet pang in her gut but she ignored it for now. One day, he would admit to her that he loved her. One day, she would prove to him that he was the most honorable man she had ever met.

She stepped forward, eating up the distance between them. Pressing her hands into his shoulders, she pulled herself up and kissed his mouth.

Those large hands of his snaked around her and slammed her against that chest. Powerful frame shuddering around her, he kissed her forehead. "I'm so sorry I hurt you with that arrogant proposal. I have become such a stranger to emotions or love that I didn't even realize what I was doing until you told me. You were right. You deserve so much more than I offered."

Hot liquid filled her eyes. Jas blinked, trying to keep the tears away. "Dmitri, are you listening? I'm not afraid anymore." She clasped his jaw, willing him to understand. "I won't break like I thought. Loving you makes me stronger, not weaker. All I want is to be with you."

"And if I do ask you to marry me again, not to protect you, but because I love you?"

"You're not playing another game with me, are you?"

"No, *pethi mou*. I've been counting the days, waiting to show you how much I need you... I thought I would show you that you've changed me already. Irrevocably."

"Wait, that's what you've been doing? Selling your bike and yacht?"

"For years, I filled myself with expensive toys that gave nothing but fleeting pleasure, with women who made me feel nothing but an echo. But with you... You have made me see that I never forgave myself. That I never thought myself worthy of anything meaningful, even though Giannis tried his hardest to tell me that it wasn't my fault that she had died."

Her chest aching for the boy he had been, Jasmine embraced him with everything she had. "It wasn't your fault, Dmitri. Just as it wasn't my duty to sacrifice my life over

Andrew's and my mother's mistakes. I want to live this life for me and I want to live it with you."

"I will wait as long as it takes. I will spend my entire life showing you that I love you." He kissed her so softly then tenderly, as if he was determined to fill all the lonely places inside her with his love. "I love you, *matia mou*. I love you so much that the world itself feels colorless without you.

"Marry me, Jas. Marry me because I want you to be mine eternally. Marry me because I need you. I need you to make me laugh, to make me feel, because I need you to love me every day for the rest of our lives."

Her heart overflowing, Jas buried her face in his chest. Fear still pulsed through her, but it was a soft echo rather than the raging growl it had been when she had come in. They would make this work; they loved each other too much for it to fail. "I love you, too, Dmitri. I want to wake up with you. I want you to help me figure out what the hell I'm going to do with my life. I want to grow old with you. I want to be a part of the family you have with Leah and Stavros. I want to spend forever with you."

"Then, you will," he said before crushing her mouth. "I promise, Jas. I will never treat you as if you were something to be protected. I will never shower you with gifts and riches instead of my heart."

"Your kisses, those are all I want," she moaned, air already an alien concept.

"Those you will have, in abundance, and in every imaginable place. Remember how you promised you would give me anything I wanted?"

Her reckless offer pulsed in the air around them, turning his eyes into a stormy sky.

"Would you dance for me one night? Just once, Jas," he said softly, but it didn't hide the guttural quality of his voice.

She braced herself, but instead of that usual wash of shame that had always flooded her, something else filled her.

Anticipation, joy, even a sense of power. Wrapping her arms around his nape, she pressed herself into his chest wantonly, reveling in the thunderstorm she could unleash in his eyes. "For the man I love? I would do anything, Dmitri."

With a smile that set her nerves on fire, Dmitri picked her up and walked over to the sitting area. And while Athens burned bright around them, he made love to her so tenderly, so softly that Jas fell in love all over again.

EPILOGUE

JASMINE WOKE UP with a huge smile on her face and then realized it was Christmas morning. Her first Christmas with Dmitri and a happy one after a long time, she thought, lazily soaking up the warmth of the Egyptian cotton sheets.

Her smile turned into a frown as she remembered her upcoming three-week trip to New York in January.

If truth be told, she had been more excited about seeing New York than her photo shoot. And now, even the attractions of the city that never slept paled in the face of not seeing Dmitri for so long.

Would Dmitri come to New York if she asked him?

Imagining all the ways she could try to convince him, she quickly showered in the en suite and dressed in a red-and-white sleeveless knee-length collared dress. She quickly braided her wet hair, applied some lip gloss and went in search of Dmitri.

The atrium gleamed in the morning sunlight, the sound of voices drawing her to the cozily contemporary kitchen.

There was no fire in the fireplace, but a four-foot Christmas tree, complete with ornaments and lights, stood near it.

Tears filled her eyes as Jas looked at it. She had spent so many Christmases trying to convince first her mother and then Andrew that they had more than most people in the world had—each other. But nothing had ever made a difference. Lost to their own weaknesses, she had never made a difference to them.

And after Andrew had been gone, she had been so lonely that even thinking of Christmas had been painful.

Strong arms encircled her from behind.

"Merry Christmas, *yineka mou*," he whispered, before turning her around and kissing her with a tender warmth that chased away some of the pain.

Wrapping her arms around his neck, Jas sank into his kiss. She nibbled at his lower lip, dueled with her tongue, poured every bit of herself into it.

And he returned everything, his hands roaming around her back, whispering promises of forever.

Holding her at arm's length, he stared at her for a long time and caught one of the tears that had escaped. "I'm so sorry about him, Jas. I wish I had saved him for you."

Jasmine shook her head, knowing that it was a habit that she had to cure Dmitri of slowly. That protective instinct was in his genes. "I wish he had saved himself, Dmitri. But no, I don't want to ruin Christmas morning with—"

"Merry Christmas, Jasmine," Leah said from behind her, a beaming smile on her lips.

Tears coming to her eyes again, this time happy ones, Jasmine returned Leah's fierce hug. And then Stavros's.

They all chattered at once and then Dmitri tugged her toward him. "Is it okay that I invited them over? I knew how happy they would be for us."

Jasmine kissed him again. She couldn't seem to stop. "Absolutely. Dmitri, I have a trip to—"

"New York, I know. If you agree, I will fly out the week after your shoot and we can see the city together. You will adore New York."

"I love you, Dmitri."

"I love you, Jas. Come, I have something for you."

While a smiling Stavros and a grinning Leah watched, he opened a small velvet box, went down on one knee and said, "Jasmine, will you marry me?"

Crying again, Jasmine nodded, absolutely incapable of speaking. Dmitri slipped the ring on her finger, a single princess-cut diamond on a plain white-gold band, his heart in his eyes.

Then he took her in his arms again and kissed her. "We'll take as long as we want, *ne*? I'm starting an inner-city program for young adults who come from broken homes and with a background of abuse and neglect. Stavros and I have already found an old building to renovate here in Athens and then we will start hiring staff.

"If, at some point in time," he stated matter-of-factly, "you have had enough of modeling and want to work on something like that, you would be more than welcome. I'm trying to cut down on my interests so that I can give it some time instead of just throwing money at it. Give a chance to someone like Giannis did for us."

Stunned into speechlessness, Jas could only stare at him.

"Jas, there is absolutely no pressure. If modeling is where your heart is, then that's what you should do. You have my support in any career you want to pursue and I will follow you around the world."

Her heart bursting to full, Jas finally spoke. "I would love to work on such a project. Dmitri, do you still have that license?"

Shock flaring in his gaze, he nodded slowly. "Jas—"

"I want to do it today, Dmitri. With Stavros and Leah as witnesses. I want to go to New York as your wife. I don't want to wait. Not when I love you so much."

When he still looked doubtful, she took his hands in hers and kissed the rough palms. "I have never wanted a big wedding or a white dress, Dmitri. I only wanted my knight. And you're it."

Dmitri lifted her off the floor in a bear hug that crushed her lungs. And then yelled the news at a stunned Leah and Stavros.

Their smiles and the way they instantly decided on their tasks made Jasmine as if like she had family again.

Breaking into supereffective mode, Leah called her assistant to have wedding gowns that she had ready delivered while Stavros made a few more arrangements.

That afternoon, they feasted on turkey, which had been ordered for her, honey-glazed ham for Leah and roast pork for Dmitri and Stavros with a variety of side delicacies. They ate delicious cinnamon-and-clove cookies drenched in honey and drank ouzo and coffee. And toasted to their new family.

When four o'clock came and a priest appeared, Jasmine felt as though she was floating on the clouds. The ivory gown Leah had chosen for her had a beaded bodice and wide skirt, and Jasmine thought it was the most beautiful she had ever looked.

Looking dashing in a black suit, Stavros walked her the little distance from her bedroom to the atrium which was filled with a golden glow.

And then there was Dmitri in a black tuxedo.

Drowning in the love that filled his gray gaze, Jasmine thought her heart would burst out of her chest. Reaching him, she smiled at him as the priest began the simple ceremony.

Jasmine was his wife. The thought repeated in his head in circles as Dmitri stood near the pool and stared at the Athens skyline. He turned the platinum band on his finger round and round, wondering if one could shatter out of joy.

Stavros joined him on silent feet and handed him a wine flute. Raising it, he said, "To Giannis."

Dmitri raised his flute and said, "To Giannis."

They remained silent, thanking the man who had made today's happiness possible in their lives.

* * * * *

#3389 BRUNETTI'S SECRET SON
Secret Heirs of Billionaires
by Maya Blake
Romeo Brunetti has found meteoric success by locking down emotion. Until a moment of recklessness years ago, when he lost himself to stunning stranger Maisie O'Connell. Now his family's legacy has returned to haunt him—*and* the child he unknowingly conceived...

#3390 BACK IN THE BRAZILIAN'S BED
Hot Brazilian Nights!
by Susan Stephens
Dante Barracca knows Karina Marcelos is the best person to organize the Gaucho Cup. But the woman he hires is a shadow of the girl he once knew. Dante will stop at nothing until he lifts the lid on Karina's secret!

#3391 DESTINED FOR THE DESERT KING
by Kate Walker
Aziza El Afarim hopes her convenient husband remembers the closeness they once shared. But Sheikh Nabil is nothing of the boy he used to be. As pressure to produce an heir mounts, is there more than duty in the marriage bed?

#3392 CAUGHT IN HIS GILDED WORLD
by Lucy Ellis
Burlesque dancer Gigi Valente will stop at nothing to defend her home. Khaled Kitaev thinks she's just another gold digger. But when her attempts to get his attention are caught on camera, the powerful Russian must usher Gigi into his world!

YOU CAN FIND MORE INFORMATION ON UPCOMING HARLEQUIN® TITLES, FREE EXCERPTS AND MORE AT WWW.HARLEQUIN.COM.

HPCNM1115RB

REQUEST YOUR FREE BOOKS!

HARLEQUIN

Presents®

2 FREE NOVELS PLUS
2 FREE GIFTS!

PASSION GUARANTEED SEDUCTION

YES! Please send me 2 FREE Harlequin Presents® novels and my 2 FREE gifts (gifts are worth about \$10). After receiving them, if I don't wish to receive any more books, I can return the shipping statement marked "cancel." If I don't cancel, I will receive 6 brand-new novels every month and be billed just \$4.30 per book in the U.S. or \$5.24 per book in Canada. That's a saving of at least 13% off the cover price! It's quite a bargain! Shipping and handling is just 50¢ per book in the U.S. and 75¢ per book in Canada.* I understand that accepting the 2 free books and gifts places me under no obligation to buy anything. I can always return a shipment and cancel at any time. Even if I never buy another book, the two free books and gifts are mine to keep forever.

106/306 HDN GHRP

Name	(PLEASE PRINT)

Address	Apt. #

City	State/Prov.	Zip/Postal Code

Signature (if under 18, a parent or guardian must sign)

Mail to the **Reader Service:**
IN U.S.A.: P.O. Box 1867, Buffalo, NY 14240-1867
IN CANADA: P.O. Box 609, Fort Erie, Ontario L2A 5X3

**Are you a current subscriber to Harlequin Presents® books
and want to receive the larger-print edition?
Call 1-800-873-8635 or visit www.ReaderService.com.**

* Terms and prices subject to change without notice. Prices do not include applicable taxes. Sales tax applicable in N.Y. Canadian residents will be charged applicable taxes. Offer not valid in Quebec. This offer is limited to one order per household. Not valid for current subscribers to Harlequin Presents books. All orders subject to credit approval. Credit or debit balances in a customer's account(s) may be offset by any other outstanding balance owed by or to the customer. Please allow 4 to 6 weeks for delivery. Offer available while quantities last.

Your Privacy—The Reader Service is committed to protecting your privacy. Our Privacy Policy is available online at www.ReaderService.com or upon request from the Reader Service.

We make a portion of our mailing list available to reputable third parties that offer products we believe may interest you. If you prefer that we not exchange your name with third parties, or if you wish to clarify or modify your communication preferences, please visit us at www.ReaderService.com/consumerchoice or write to us at Reader Service Preference Service, P.O. Box 9062, Buffalo, NY 14240-9062. Include your complete name and address.

"Well," he said, "it was very refreshing to meet you, Ms. Tennent."

"It was very daunting to meet you." Libby smiled. "Well, it was at first."

"And how about now?"

His hands went to her hips, the move sexy and suggestive as he framed where their minds were. Libby had a sudden urge to be lifted by him, to wrap her legs around him.

"I'm very daunted," she admitted, "though the middle bit was fun."

It *was* daunting only because she was about to be kissed by the devil.

He didn't test the water, he didn't start slowly, he just lowered his head from a great distance and Libby got the most thorough kissing of her life.

This was his kiss to her, his mouth said. It wasn't a dance of their mouths. He didn't even lead, he simply took over, tasting her, stilling her, making her body roar into flame with his mouth.

His kiss had her hot, right there in the street, but the only movement he allowed was to let her hands reach for his chest. Then, when he'd coiled her so tight, he released her mouth. He'd let her glimpse a fraction of what being held by him felt like and then he cruelly removed the pleasure.

She sucked in the summer night air while craving his mouth again.

"Bed," Daniil said.

"I don't…" Libby halted. What had she been about to say—that she didn't want to?

Well, yes, she did.

Since the age of eight, dancing had come first, which had meant self-discipline.

In everything.

How nice to stand here on the brink of making a decision based purely on her own needs and wants right now, at this moment.

And she did want.

So she chose to say yes when the wisest choice might have been to decline.

"Bed." Libby nodded and then blinked at her response. She didn't retract it, but her voice was rueful when she spoke next. "I am so going to regret this in the morning."

"Only if you expect me to love you by then."

Third warning bell.

She could turn and walk away.

"Oh, no," Libby said, and in that at least she was wise.

"Then there's no reason for regret."

Don't miss
THE PRICE OF HIS REDEMPTION
by Carol Marinelli, available December 2015 wherever
Harlequin Presents® books and ebooks are sold.

www.Harlequin.com